Praise for *Beaut*

With his debut novel, Donald Morrill shows that prose and poetry can become indistinguishable on the page just as beauty and tragedy are often indistinguishable in our lives. This is a punchy, finely written novel driven by a fierce determination to condense our humanity to the written word.

—Wiley Cash, author of *The Last Ballad* and
A Land More Kind Than Home

Donald Morrill's first novel is a compelling meta-narrative of an exposed and broken heart, illusive truth and seductive lies, and how loved ones suffer and benefit from this daily and inevitable symmetry. Jill Lundgrove's confessions are both elliptical and luminous, and I couldn't stop reading.

—Darnell Arnoult, author of *Sufficient Grace*
and *Galaxie Wagon*

Beaut is as sharp and luminous a novel as I have read this year, a meditation on the terrible beauty and grace of the stories we tell ourselves and the legacies we leave behind.

—Taylor Brown, author of *Gods of Howl Mountain*
and *The River of Kings*

Morrill's debut novel is tenderness wrapped in mystery. *Beaut* riddles our deepest beliefs about maturity and loyalty, its drive as real as love itself.

—Edie Meidav, author of
Kingdom of the Young and *Lola, California*

BEAUT

BEAUT

— A NOVEL —

Donald Morrill

BLAIR

Typeset in Arno by Copperline Book Services, Inc.

Blair is an imprint of Carolina Wren Press.

*The mission of Carolina Wren Press is to seek out, nurture,
and promote literary work by new and underrepresented writers,
including women and writers of color.*

Library of Congress Cataloging-in-Publication Data
Names: Morrill, Donald, 1955– author.
Title: Beaut : a novel / Donald Morrill.
Description: Durham, NC : Carolina Wren Press, [2017]
Identifiers: LCCN 2017048738 (print) | LCCN 2017055907 (ebook) |
ISBN 9780932112750 (ebook) | ISBN 9780932112743
(softcover : acid-free paper)
Subjects: LCSH: Dysfunctional families—Fiction. | Single mothers—
Fiction. | Widows—Fiction. | Domestic fiction.
Classification: LCC PS3563.O8737 (ebook) |
LCC PS3563.O8737 B43 2017 (print) | DDC 813/.54—dc23
LC record available at https://lccn.loc.gov/2017048738

T

HE MONSTER CALLED my cell phone this morning, demanding money.

That's how he asks when he's in trouble. He doesn't know where I'm living right now. I felt the impulse to pick up and tell him, but I've let Petey think I've promised not to.

Petey wants to bring charges against him, for burning my house down. I was in the hospital at the time, just after New Year's. You could say I was lucky my granddaughter, Kate, found me lying in the hallway. She'd stopped by on her way to classes at the community college. The Monster was home, too. Petey rants at me over and over that the Monster wouldn't even go in the ambulance with me, that he just stood there stoned-staring, licking an ice cream cone while the emergency team shocked me back. And then he went into his room.

It's true that if Kate hadn't happened by the house when she did, I'd be dead. (I almost wrote that I'd be with you. Not true. Not ever. I'd just be in your realm, if the dead share a realm.) I can see the Monster standing in the doorway, blank as a bull's-eye. I know at that moment neither of us has a chance. Kate used to have a knee-hugging love for him, until he and her mother separated for the last time and she hit puberty, and the pain came between them all. He used to take her fishing when she was a child.

I don't remember a thing about my collapse. I'd felt shaky beforehand, a little queasy, flu-ish, maybe. Then I was out. There was surgery, of course, right away, and the recovery room—so cold that room, and then the phone call. I was swimming in and out of the situation, you could say, given the painkillers and whatnot. The Monster was shouting at me through the receiver, crying and high. He needed money and he needed it now, and if I didn't give it to him, he'd torch everything.

It's not as though he hadn't threatened this before. Or stolen pieces of my furniture to pawn. Or written bad checks from my account and even from Ray's a year after he'd died. I wonder if one of his so-called friends heard his threat and decided to make it happen. More than one of those cretins have used him for their fun. He's sentimental, the Monster is. He doesn't learn.

But it's not clear any fire was deliberately set. The whole thing could have been sparked by a cigarette fallen from an ashtray. He was lucky to be away and not passed out there.

This morning's rant finally wound down to a pause, as though a revelation were in store, and then, "I'm trying my best, Mom, I really am. You know that. . . . I'm sorry . . . Ma, I can't keep sleeping in Fred's car! C'mon, pick up!"

He must be quite lonely, wherever he is.

I know, Petey has a point. The Monster is thirty-eight years old and has no business being so afraid, or being so skillful at it.

THE TRAFFICKERS SEPARATE the baby camel from its mother and truck it to a rendezvous point across the frontier. Then they load the mother with their contraband and send her off. No matter how implacable the terrain, even if she's leading a train of other camels, she makes her way toward her offspring. But if you were to come across her in the middle of her trek, you wouldn't find any guilty parties to arrest. Only the cargo, slung on her hump, and her pathetic determination.

That's supposed to be the beauty of the situation, I guess . . . and it is, if you're a smuggler.

Petey slipped this newspaper story under one of my fridge magnets a couple of years ago. He thought it made his usual point about me and the Monster. I mention it because I have to start somewhere, since it seems I'm starting again . . . because of everything that's happened with the Monster, and because Ollie Picks may actually ask me to marry him.

Probably I mention it because I've thought of you often these days. What a hump across the years I've become! So who's hurt if I talk to you, or toward you . . . or whatever this is . . . just now, for a start? Since it appears I have no motivation to talk much to myself alone, even while I'm in great need of reckoning. There's not a love in my life today I can trust for it.

I'm sure you don't already know these things, though sometimes I've pretended you do. Even if there is some Other Side, where you could be, why would you be informed of anything that occurs here? Why would you care?

Unless you're being punished.

Or I am.

Hardly.

You don't know anything.

You never will.

———

Okay. Let's try this again.

The Monster, Monte, is mine. I mean I gave birth to him and to Carla.

Petey and April were my brother Phil's, until they were eight and six.

Petey has always been devoted to me, which is still a problem. He doesn't approve. He thinks he hates the Monster. And now he resents the idea of Ollie. He'll do anything for me as long as he approves. I don't know how many more times I can afford to hurt him.

Petey can be handy around the house. He's always been eager that way, and this still gives us something in common. He can do for me. I do for him by letting him.

But I know, too, I can peel his last good nerve. I can see it when he puffs a little as he reaches into the toilet tank to hook up the chain on the stopper. He wonders why I couldn't bother just enough to put it on. This question probably goes back a long way. Most everything does, more and more now. Petey's adoptive father, Ray, couldn't put that chain on, though he could put it on his list of things to do. And the Monster . . . if he wasn't high, the Monster could replace the whole fixture and rewire the lights and repaint the walls and make it a showcase.

But Petey delivers. I think he'd be pleased to hear me say that. He visits, before or after work, though not every day since I'm placed, for the moment, in this new, clean, awful little apartment facing—what else?—a cornfield.

I think his wife Jane resents his stopping by. She's always been jealous, and with some justification. But she benefits. He puts in those long hours at the dairy (he manages the accounting there) and she parades the kids in that special school. She likes to be seen pushing a designer baby stroller among other moms pushing identical strollers. I admire her appetite, if nothing else. It's helped to make Petey as successful as he is. It might also give him most of whatever happiness he has, though I don't think that's much.

I should be out walking myself, now, maybe not with the decrepits at the mall, but somewhere. The doctor wants it, since I've gotten this pacemaker. (I call it my peacemaker. Always with the wishful thinking, me.) I should be out instead of trying to write down things I've said, if at all, under my breath, halfway, alone in the car, in the shower.

Maybe you understood (but only a little, I think) that, eventually, talking about your life is talking about mistakes. If you live long enough, you have to attend your own charm school, or no one will give a damn about you, except to pay their respects.

My mouth hurts when I think of becoming an old woman in a flowered housecoat, smelling as fragile as yellowed newspaper and about as worthy of attention.

I'm a liar, I know. Carla has declared that enough in nearly everything she's done. And you told me that, too.

On some of my worst days afterward, I could still hear it.

Probably this is a good place to stop, for now.

'M SIXTY-SIX. CAN you believe it?
You would be seventy.
But then that wouldn't be you, would it?
It's very quiet in this room this morning.

I JUST FIRED UP my computer and see I stopped two days ago with the quiet. I don't think I'll ever get used to it.

It seems terrible sometimes, the silence . . . and the sunlight, which I'm supposed to be grateful for now. (The phone will ring at the dinner hour and be the first sound of the day. And there will be some girl with that scratchy, tickled bellybutton voice introducing herself as an assistant loan officer and trying to read her script. I know she's probably a mother, too. And a fool.)

But the silence here isn't the same as it was in my house. There, it usually crept over me when the Monster was away bingeing with the cretins, and those four times he actually moved out, twice with Sheila and the kids, once for a year and a half.

Now sometimes I go out just to hear the wind, or the traffic. Putting on the TV or a CD is too much an admission of weakness.

Ollie smells that silence on me, I think.

He's fifty-four. I shouldn't worry about this. He tells me I have a remarkable chin and shockingly smooth skin. And I do, for my age, of course. Always for that. It almost seems to be in exchange for losing the best remainder of my bust, which was once ample enough (remember?). Dear, it's sunk into a couple of sad socks in the last ten years. One day I looked up into the mirror and even my best turn and most upright push-out couldn't shoo away the facts. I wouldn't have given that or any part of me a chance of aching well again and scaring me, not with anyone, let alone Ollie. But then it's easy to forget how many people of all ages are lying down alone right now with their hands between their legs. We forget a lot, we do. Sometimes we think a subject is closed just before it's truly opened.

Ollie is solid chested but thin, though he was probably much thinner when he was younger. I haven't seen any photographs. He says he hasn't kept them. All his family is dead, he says, though he corresponds with someone named Laura Aussoway in Santa Clara, California. I saw the stack of letters on his dresser. (It's funny he doesn't use email with her . . . or maybe he does?) Anyway, he lives in a rooming house (do they still call them that?) near the university. He likes having the students around, even though, he says, there's always someone leaving for good. The place is dreadful, with a gas heater along the baseboards and fluorescent abstract student paintings in the stairwell. I suppose this sort of probable poverty has encouraged me about him all along. Maybe Ollie was once able to seduce a coed or two (they, wanting the experience of an older man, and he with the silvering mane), but I'm not even sure of that. The most he can do now, it seems, is impress them with his omelets on a Saturday morning, those who are up early enough and not too hung over.

"You know very well your beauty," he told me, on that afternoon at his room, which I now call Afternoon Number One, "but let me try to articulate how I know it . . ."

I wanted Ollie for sex, once I realized that's what he was going to try. Yes. That's how we began. He seemed not to have been touched for a long time, longer than it had been for me. I wanted to see if I had any touches left.

I taught high school for five years, in my later forties, and I felt I did it well, at times, though teaching is often as much abuse as it is gift-giving, and I finally managed to coerce Ray into letting me stop. I've always loved Tolstoy's *War and Peace* (your recommendation, right?), but we were never allowed to teach it, even to seniors. It was too long, we were told. Instead we always faced *The Old Man and the Sea*. I used to think how false it was, that book, and I know it is, even though I have my big Ollie-fish, untouched, beside my little boat now.

I can't marry him. I'd lose Ray's pension. Though that's about sixth down on my list of good excuses. Petey isn't thinking of this when he has that look on his face that means he doesn't dare say what he's thinking: Ollie is a loser who only wants your monthly check. Amazing, that fear of the truth in your mind, as though Petey's mind could keep any secret from me.

L ET ME SEE.

Carla moved to New Mexico almost ten years ago and came back last month to verify my recovery but, really, to have it out with me. I couldn't be shocked since I hadn't seen her in some time.

She said that her therapist had helped her come to some conclusions.

"You know I've been mad at you for years," she said.

"Why, dear?" I asked. (You'd be surprised at my gentle tone, the blandness of it. Years of practice, believe me.)

"I think you know why," she said.

I could have guessed, it's true. Carla has never forgiven me for really taking charge of Ray's care in his last months. She thinks I was keeping him from her.

There was a moment when I went to the bed, not long before he passed. Her eyes were on me like claws. She couldn't have known how I felt. I don't blame her. Ray was about to take his final breath, about to turn golden for a moment, as he did, as you did. It was about to happen, at last, but this time I'd be present.

Growing up, Carla never gave me any trouble. It seemed like she had a window to stare out of everywhere she went. I was grateful for that, considering how overwhelmed I was in those first years when Ray and I suddenly had four kids instead of two.

That should have been my clue on Carla. I never gave my mother any trouble, either.

"You didn't want any of us," Carla said, as though it were the solution to some problem. Maybe it was. "Not just them, but us, too."

Carla is forgiving me, often and with great effort. Every day, I imagine.

"I don't know what you mean," I said. (I guess I'd forgotten all I thought I'd learned about saying the truth.)

You have to know that, for years, I made sure Carla could concern herself only with being a pretty girl. Like me before I met you.

I hoped that would make up for her being surprised so awfully by Petey and April.

CAN I SAY it here?

The kids made me love Ray more than I might have. This seems, now, enough justification for twenty-nine years of marriage. He was not a lovable man, though he wasn't mean. Merely shy in certain ways.

What am I getting at?

After you, I left Chicago right away and came back to Des Moines. My parents thought I was still working for S&H Green Stamps and that I'd simply gotten homesick. They may have believed I'd returned with second thoughts about my broken engagement to Terry Jenkins, who was still floating around town and even called me once. I let them wonder. I stayed with them a week, sleeping in my old twin bed, and then I rented a little dump on Walnut Avenue, not far from the Capitol building and the garden with the Japanese bell. I took a filing job at *Midwest Farmer* magazine. I didn't care how menial it was. I met Ray about two years later.

None of it seems quite real, of course. Since it was. And is, as much as it can be.

I never told my parents about you. I never told anyone. And, amazingly, no one called me from Chicago, or anywhere, about you. (I kept waiting for that call, scared of it. I guess you never told anyone substantial about me, and our little party crew must have thought we'd split long before. But what about the landlady? Lila. Wasn't that her name? She and I talked once in a while. She knew me.)

I've never told anyone since.

It's turned out to be simpler than I could have imagined, though maybe not easy.

At first, I kept quiet because I didn't want to be . . . what?

Implicated. That's it.

Remember, I was running for my life. And who can understand how far that might be? I'm still not certain it can be done.

At that age (how old I thought I was at twenty-three, already fearful of spinsterhood despite the bohemian poses I'd learned from you!), the years are bigger than they've been since. So much went into a month, a day. And I had to shut you out of each.

If I could have paid more attention to the full future, if I'd had more courage somehow, and if they'd have let a woman sign up then, I might have joined the Peace Corps, which was founded about that time or a little after. It seems just one more missed opportunity now, my own French Foreign Legion. And don't we all have legions and legions? What would I have become by building fish ponds in Liberia? I should have left Des Moines again.

You would have loved the idea of the Peace Corps, even if you would have damned my motives for joining, or your own motives.

So I didn't disappear, but part of me had more or less vanished and wouldn't be coaxed back.

It took me a long time (until June 4, 1979, to be exact, in a canoe on Lake Panorama) to admit I'd meant it when I told you I loved you. Can you believe it?

Before that, I had to call it something else, to survive it.

You wanted me forever. Didn't you?

How does it feel?

I loved Ray. He deserved my best more often. We were desperate together, opposite to the way you and I were desperate, I like to think. I would never have left him.

That's not where I'd intended to end up today.

I was trying to talk about walking with April on Blue Jay Trail. It's one of the defunct railroad lines they've turned into a bike and hike—a straight, paved strip for thirty miles south, past Indianola, though I never go much beyond the crummy park a mile and a half from here, and we didn't, this morning.

Long and straight—that's Iowa, most of the time. That's what we like to say, both its lovers and its haters.

Since it's her name month, and really quite warmer and sweeter than usual, April came over in delight. She's good this way, checking with me first, to see if I truly want company. Unlike Petey, who makes me feel like he's walking me, she actually bothers to enjoy the scenery. She and Howard have been farming near Runnels, forty-five minutes from here, for seventeen years. Ever since they got married out of college. I think it pleases her to be amid nature she doesn't have to worry over. It also doesn't hurt her to get some aerobic exposure herself; she's gotten so big in the last five or six years.

April doesn't want me to die, of course, but she wishes me dead so we don't have to talk, or not talk, as is our practice while saying words to each other. Walking together now and then helps, as does shopping, or maybe watching her oldest son in left field for his high school team . . . until the day she can talk to me like I imagine she talks to Ray now. Or until I talk to her like I talk to you here.

Until then, we're kind, if sometimes impolite.

She visits Ray at Laurel Hill Cemetery. She opposed my suggestion that he be cremated and his ashes spread at Lake Panorama. (He hadn't left instructions. That was one to-do list he didn't make.) She's the same age as the Monster, and yet she seems younger. She was twenty-seven when Ray died, but you'd have thought she was eleven the way she wailed. Of course, it was another loss. She's sentimental like the Monster is, except she turns it outward. That's why none of us want for homemade jellies and venison jerky and battery-operated craft kit knick-knack clutter. April is a constant Christmas. She doesn't go near anyone without gifts, and her thoughtfulness can't be refused.

No one knows where her birth mother, Lucy, is buried. I assume she's long dead, given her ferocious boozing. I only met her once, not long after she and Phil married, at a family reunion picnic. They were drunk and young and very funny. Phil lost track of her in California, sometime in 1968. He hasn't seen Petey and April since he gave them up (or dumped them, depending on how you view it) in 1970. You can see the problem there, his not returning, though I've mostly considered it a gift.

Maybe Lucy got big like April has raising corn and hogs and three kids on eight hundred inherited acres with a man whom she once told me was homely enough to be good to her. The weight problem might be a clue that April toys with, though I don't mention it, since she jokes too much about her hurts that don't directly involve me.

"Same chore, different day," she laughs, about having to "put out" for Howard.

Even with the girlish pimples (a side effect of her hormone treatment), she looks very much like Phil. Which is to say that, until she put on the weight, she and I often passed for mother and daughter among the ignorant.

I guess I'm worried about her heart, as though she could have inherited mine.

April, I'm certain, worries about having to care for me if I live long enough and become, to use her term, a "half-gomer." Jane would never let Petey take me in. I can't say I would allow it, as if I would have a choice then. Fortunately, April will fight to keep me from the clutches of geezer care. Several years ago she worked at one of those places, Somerset Village, right along Blue Jay Trail.

"At least you're not in the Laotian suite—yet," she says, when she detects discouragement in me that needs shooing away.

She means that Laotian woman she told me about, almost a full-gomer, lying on the floor at Somerset, screeching all night in a language even her children didn't recognize, and weeping, her mind like a tiny cinder that wouldn't be blessed with snuffing out.

———

That's not where I wanted to end up today, either. But I need to take a shower and get on with the afternoon.

THE MONSTER HAS called two more times this week, yesterday and this morning. I've resisted answering, though I turned the phone off after that second call ending with "So you're gonna let him throw me out just like that . . . Okay then. It'll be on your head!"

His tears had real fear in them for a change, as if he were eight again and had just fled the deep end of Teachout swimming pool, hacking up water, scampering to park himself between my knees for half the afternoon. (How could he be that boy, or the one who became an all-conference high school pitcher in his sophomore year, a boy the college scouts would be watching?)

I've also resisted telling Petey about the calls, though I've mentioned them to April and Ollie. If Petey needs to think of me as a camel, so be it. But he doesn't need undue encouragement in that regard. (If anything, I'm more like one of the students in that pickpocket school in Shanghai that was busted recently. They honed their skills by trying to snatch a coin from a pan of scalding water without splashing or burning their fingers.)

My children have their lives, and the truth is, at least as far as my relations with Ollie are concerned, they think my life should be over. They wouldn't admit it, and they might not even be aware of it, but they believe if I want what they want out of life, that's wrong, because they're younger. They assume there's a statute of limitations on trying to live happily, with what you like. I've had my chance, now they get theirs—as though everyone only gets a discernible number of chances and no more.

The Monster clings most to these notions. Odd, really, since as a child, he tore across everyone's boundaries, crashing into the lap of the handiest grown-up, or shouting "Kiss! Kiss!" and firing himself at people. Relentless. And how many came to despise him for it! You could sense their shame at discovering they could crave revenge on a kid. (I would see Ray, sometimes to my ugly delight, fighting several malodorous urges.) And, yes, people would cast a glancing appeal my way, that I might bring the creature to heel.

With the exception of a few who deserved a dose of "Monster love," I tried to rescue most people. That task, of course, was one of those big wheels in parenthood that eventually grind right down through your forehead and split your will. What else in life did the Monster have to do besides teach me that? He also managed to convince me, even if I knew better, that in calling him off I'd actually hurt him and he wouldn't forget it, in spite of himself.

I always fight the tendency of children to wall a mother away from everyone her age. You'd be surprised how many women hate such gestures toward freedom . . . or maybe you wouldn't. They treat themselves like a pebble they've thrown in a well and never want to hear hit bottom.

My mother never allowed herself to be sequestered by us, and she, more skillful or blessed than I, managed to make the three of us each feel we were her favorite.

Still we tried to wall her up, over and over, to the end. That's clear now. Kids can't help it.

The Monster would make Petey seem un-possessive, if he could organize his impulses. But, really, his mess is beyond owning me. Possession was just the first phase of it. Messes like that are more patient and efficient than love.

I SPENT LAST NIGHT at Ollie's. Night Number Seven, now duly registered.

I've begun keeping track, yes, since it's apparent we're weird this way. Six afternoons and now seven nights at his room since we met last October.

Sound familiar?

It's not the same.

Ollie once folded towels for a living. He's driven a taxi in L.A. and managed a kennel in Winnipeg. Now he works online in his room, as some type of troubleshooter for a security firm in Boston. (His equipment is the only up-to-date item in sight.) He says he spends so much time there he would rather go elsewhere for the rest of his waking hours.

That impulse toward elsewhere, however, is not the refined agent he would like. Just as he hasn't accumulated the customary toys and trophies, he's sometimes manhandled by the possibility of multiple destinations. That's why he ends up staying in and reading, and rereading, so much.

He's uncertain, too, what the kids in his rooming house think of his bedding down with me.

I could tell him: Gross!

You could almost hear it when we came down to the kitchen this morning and found the two girls—Chelsea and . . . Jennifer?—from the room next to his slouching over their coffee and bio notebooks.

I thought of my granddaughter Kate and wondered what lesson the appearance of a semi-crone willfully in a man's blue robe at seven a.m. might impart to her. Nonplussed, those girls seemed, despite their severely pierced eyebrows and noses, and eager to flee as we do from a truth that puts us to squirming.

"Hi," they said, and made a space at the table. We even shook hands.

But I wouldn't let them go so easily. It had taken me some courage, after all, to come downstairs like that.

"Spare a cigarette?" I asked. Chelsea pushed forward a pack of those vacant super lights, menthol to boot. Ollie's eyebrows turned a somersault since I'm supposed to have quit smoking, and mostly have. As he heated up the skillet, I blocked the girls' escape by rolling out the questions. Where are you from? What's your major? Isn't that hard? Do you have a job, too? Boyfriends?

"Guys . . ." Jennifer sighed, and they both chuckled.

It occurs to me now they might have been an item.

"Yes, they can be so stupid," I added, blowing a little smoke in Ollie's direction.

At that moment I simply thought the longer I sat with these two, the more opportunity they would have to grasp that I'm worth getting to know. I thought they must learn sooner rather than later that older people are not their parents. And that they themselves are older people in the making.

After eleven sometimes-sweet post-Ray years, I take a silly adult education class and meet this odd man, Ollie. And now

I'm seated in this sloping, modestly grimy kitchen, wondering if these two quite decent, slightly zaftig girls from Minnesota heard Ollie's squeaky headboard last night, a squeak I'm proud of. I want to proclaim to them: This man didn't desert me when I went into the hospital, he touches me, everywhere, and he likes it, he wants to, he even touches the hard place just below my left collarbone, my badge, three wires and a battery, and he frightens me.

I wanted to shake them with these things and more.

Instead, maybe I should have offered observations on fruit-flavored lubricants?

"Well," I said, after they begged off for class. "That was a real . . . *triumph!*"

Ollie kissed my nape and served up Egg Beaters (low cholesterol).

If he were younger, I could imagine he's finally getting the instruction from the older woman he clearly craves and can use on the next woman in line, the real woman for him, the one who benefits as we all most often benefit—unknowingly.

I LOST MY HOUSE six months ago. I lost my husband eleven years ago today.

What can this possibly mean?

In the newspaper there's a story of a small girl back East with several broken bones, at different stages of healing.

And we . . . no, not us, but the current government of this country, just a wealthy gang of thieves . . . they're still invading Iraq. Some soldiers shot up an Iraqi family in a van. The father is quoted as saying he saw the heads of his two daughters come off.

There's an article, too, about a town in Georgia that wants to reinstate segregated proms . . . Are we heading back to the age of Emmett Till? Or Roy Cohn, that old, lying buggerer?

Where am I?

Most everything of my house is gone, except three boxes of letters and pictures and papers that were in the farthest corner of the garage. They're in a closet at Petey's now. (I couldn't trust April with them. She's always been a snoop.) I don't think I'll ever go through them. I guess I don't want to verify what the flames have taken for sure.

I don't visit Laurel Hill. Whatever that is below the screwed-down coffin lid is not Ray. After so much neglect from me since he died (at least April might think of it as neglect), I don't know where he is.

Or my parents.

Or you.

Here, maybe?

At the mall today, on the wall beside our table at Friday's among all the metal soda signs and antique advertisements and paraphernalia plastering the place with nostalgic cheer, there was a real photo of a handsome middle-aged couple, Italians, they seemed, and probably from the late nineteenth century.

Obviously, it had been intended to hang above a mantel, and no doubt it had once. For how long?

But here it was now, at lunch with the likes of Ollie and me.

Not where it will end up, of course.

The past, it was supposed to say, and say nothing more.

That's why I hate this world sometimes.

SHOULDN'T REREAD the previous entry before I start writing. Rereading distracts. And who wants to hear how repetitive she is? Today is another day, right?

I can be optimistic. Those stunted Georgians aside, you'd be surprised, actually, at how common it is to see blacks and whites together now, as friends, or dating. Marriage, too. There was a group at the mall yesterday, all about sixteen years old, and every color and flavor, practically. The boys swimming in their giant-sized clothes, and the girls, every one, bursting from the tiniest tops and bottoms they could sneak themselves into . . . wearing the heaviest, most elaborate makeup. On balance, it seems an improvement, even if the girls still appeared to hover and fight like hummingbirds for the boys' attention, not at all aware how long they'll be willing to serve it.

So, utopia comes a little closer. And kids are still afraid of their desires in a way we, I think, would recognize.

My optimism has also charmed Ollie.

A couple of weeks ago, I dragged him to a peace protest at the foot of the Capitol building. We were nervous about it. Neither of us had ever done anything like that before. There were only maybe a hundred of us, but the TV chopper circled overhead, and cops were everywhere. A young black man with a bullhorn led us in chants: *What do we want? Justice! When do we want it? Now!* And *George Bush, you can't hide! We charge you with genocide!*

Ollie could see he had a live one with me. As if he didn't already know.

Afterward, he said, grinning slightly and with real gratitude in his voice, "Who *are* you?"

The protest was only a few blocks from the apartment I'd gotten after coming back from you in Chicago. That neighborhood was long ago bulldozed, of course. That apartment was a terrible little place, with a fold-down ironing board in the living room wall that I never used.

I felt foolish chanting, and I could see Ollie did, too. Next to us stood a rumpled, lonely-looking man with a poster that said *Iraq Is Another Wounded Knee.* I could hear my own voice somehow separate from the others. But I was also thinking that I've been a coward most of my life when faced with clear wrongs like this latest pack of lies and military arrogance. I kept thinking of those photographs on the Internet of nudists around the world lying out on hillsides and sea shores in the shape of peace symbols.

Silly as it might be, I needed to do something for once, however futile.

April told me that Carla actually hooted and clapped when she heard about it. Of course, Carla doesn't believe me, or in me. She's not big on trusting me, for all her occasional candor. We've never talked about that, of course. It's one of those windows she stares out of, away from me. She'd rather thump me like she did a couple of years ago when I cashed in the last of Ray's profit sharing to pay for the Monster's return to rehab.

"I'm not supporting his addictions through you," she'd shouted. "If you give him everything and he bankrupts you, don't look to me for help! You can live in the street!"

From one perspective, I probably deserved it.

Carla, it turns out, has changed her last name.

April let that tidbit slip a few weeks ago. But she won't reveal when the change was made or what the name is. She promised Carla, and April always keeps the back half of her broken promises. So I'll have to wait for the chance to ask Petey.

T ISN'T ALL silence around this apartment. The dog next door is dragging his metal bowl across the slab patio. The cornfield beyond the street is still brown but getting attention from two tractors. All the years with Ray in the farm implement business, and I still can't tell you what those tractors are doing just now. I guess I wanted to remain a city girl, as much as I could be one in Des Moines.

When I became pregnant by Ray, it was too late. I had my doubts, but I'd used up my decisiveness, and Ray wanted the baby (which turned out to be the Monster) so badly. We sat in a coffee shop next door to Sumner Pontiac, and he did a monthly budget on a napkin. He was trying to show me we could make it financially. That meant a lot to him. He was ten years older, thirty-seven, and established at the dealership, and he would be better established. He already had his own house (though we sold it and got the bigger place on the cul-de-sac). I'd found his maturity and assurance attractive, I'll admit it; that's why we began dating in the first place. He could be infectious when he wanted to move people. I think he was afraid he wasn't going to have a family of his own. He was still a farm boy from Guthrie County, but all grown up and maybe even thinking he was getting on. He was pushing against his shyness, too. I learned how to do that from him, finally, not from you.

Those numbers on a napkin were a comfort to me, an inspiration, just because they could be added and subtracted. And because Ray held my hands over them and gazed at me with tenderness and pride (with the same amazed strength, really, that I'd come to see when I'd praise him, say, for putting up an especially unwieldy Christmas tree). I realized then I wasn't going to have to sit in my dump on Walnut Avenue with Eleanor from the art department at Ace Printing (she's the one who introduced Ray and me, by the way) . . . I wasn't going to have to sit there again and decide not to tell her my condition and maybe lose her friendship if I asked her if she knew someone able to help me get out of it.

Anyway, it's all legal now, for the moment, despite the kooks of virtue who scream murder and want it outlawed and think they mean well.

————

Once you were gone, I wasn't strong enough to follow through alone, that's why I ended it. I had to be realistic.

(Odd now, that caused me to be more alone, and yet less, too.)

You'd been so troubled, so ill, really . . . lovely as you were. Anyone could see that, now.

It scared me to think how much of that chaos the child might inherit.

What does it take to be faithful? My mother, I think, relished being a mother. I know many women who have. I thought I probably would be. I'm not saying it isn't gratifying.

I must also be saying it's turned out to be none of your business. You're one of the few I can say that to.

AGAIN, I SEE myself collapsed in the hallway of my house, twitching and generally racking. (I don't know if I was actually twitching. I haven't asked Kate. I must be imagining it because the doctor said I was most likely suffering from severe arrhythmia at that point. I didn't really flatline in earnest until the medics arrived, lucky for me. That's usually what kills people. They don't know they have a problem until it's too late.) But I see myself there with the Monster licking his ice cream cone. However much he might have been zonked, I wonder if he scooped up that cone and let me lie there twitching and dying until Kate happened to show up. Maybe he'd rather have me on that floor than lying with Ollie.

I'd had Ollie to the house only twice before, but we were also meeting regularly for coffee or a trip to the art center, or whatnot, and though I hadn't spoken to the Monster about it, we were already on Afternoon Number Four. It was clear. Big changes might finally be coming to the house, and the Monster resented it.

Of course, I hadn't told Ollie anything about the Monster's lab junk in the basement or the cretins staying down there against my orders. I didn't want to queer my chances for us, if there were chances, by dumping more complications on him.

And I hadn't been down to the basement myself in over a year, not since I'd gotten the gumption one morning to tell the cretins to leave and opened the door and took one step, and up came this voice, like a cool tongue in my ear, "Mrs. Lundgrove, go back. It's not a healthy atmosphere."

That was the alpha cretin, Cane Toad, they called him. He's probably the father of the Monster's littlest boy, Henry, who's Cane Toad in miniature. (But the Monster has always claimed Henry as his own, part of the Monster's sweetness that's given me hope.) April insisted it was common knowledge that Cane Toad was a crack refiner and had killed a man with his car. He seemed to me just the usual kind of parasite the Monster attracts.

I'll say it. I'd been a prisoner in my own house for a long time. Carla and Petey had been preaching that one to me for years. Even Ray, as he was finally giving everything up to the cancer, alluded to how he thought the Monster would take me over. He'd kept the Monster's worst habits out of the house, though the Monster would return to us from time to time, when he and his ex, Sheila, would lose another apartment to a spate of co-bingeing. We had them and the kids with us more than once.

I knew I was a prisoner, of my own design, you could say. I'd witnessed the Monster through three rehabs. I could comprehend the lexicon of dependence. But that day Cane Toad warned me away, I began to finally realize.

That night, they knocked around extra much. They'd brought women in, too. Whores, more or less, weird creatures, some of them kids, really, and at least one viney battle-ax, in sequined jeans, almost my age, with eyes that seemed pinned on. She laughed into my face as they trooped downstairs. I put a chair against my bedroom door. Cane Toad had already shown an aptitude for scaring me, and his creepy request at the basement stairs was just the conclusive gesture. I think the Monster eventually learned the ways from him.

Some of those nights they'd play their crap metal music, and some nights they were very quiet, but I lay awake, certain my bedroom door would burst open with Cane Toad or one of the others. I started keeping a kitchen knife on the night stand. More than once, I almost called Petey but then didn't because he's so confrontational. We didn't need that.

Things declined.

The Monster stopped working, little by little, as he would when a binge took hold, and then he was fired, as usual. But he was on something else now. He was becoming something else. It seems now that I was, too.

He'd take my car keys and leave me stranded overnight. When I asked Petey to drive me somewhere, I'd tell him I'd loaned my car.

The Monster also locked me in the garage one afternoon. I didn't make a fuss because I didn't want the neighbors brought in on the situation. I also didn't need the police, though Petey was always declaring that the law was precisely what was required.

One day, the Monster slammed down the phone and threw his fist through the linen closet door. Another time, when I didn't have any money for him (he claimed he needed it to get his tools out of hock), I hid in the bathroom and he kicked the door in. There I was, sitting on the edge of the tub. He was so thin then, and panting. He roared, that was it, a roar. He swept the cosmetics off the vanity and fired a can of hair spray at me. It bounced around the shower stall. I didn't stand up. I didn't want him to notice me any further. His eyes were flat, like a fish.

Those weren't the only incidents. There were others, as dangerous, I see now. The Monster always came to me afterward, weeping, mortified. So much had added up in him.

It occurs to me now (and I have to say, it's left me staring for a few minutes at the cursor, wincing, really) the Monster would clutch me and shudder with tears, a jag of bawling and a thousand apologies. Whatever resolve I had about him beforehand I put aside for the moment because it seemed I couldn't forgive him enough, nothing could. We have a long history of making up, but this was off the chart for us. He was so tall and remorseful, the sorrys spooling out of him in a whisper, endless, and he held me so tightly he seemed about to explode, like he might break me in half at any moment, like he might suddenly squeeze us both to death to get it out of himself. I'm not joking.

What stopped me a few minutes ago is that it reminded me of you at times.

But I can't go there now. I really can't.

All the escalation with the Monster made me more afraid for Petey. Though strong, he's much shorter and smaller than the Monster. He gave up on the Monster after the first rehab didn't hold. That would have been 1994. Ray had been gone two years, and I was happy to let Petey step in and fix us all. He's two years older than the Monster and has tried, now and then, to be a big brother to him, for me. But Petey couldn't abide the Monster mouthing all the clinical terms and self-improvement buzzwords and not advancing an iota. He wanted the Monster to become like him, I think. They were in their later twenties, and Petey, dependable Petey, was already married and working, as Jane wished, at the dairy. The Monster hated Jane and her influence by proxy even more.

At least, that's how I excused his unwillingness and failures then.

Petey would never admit it (because it would make him think he was more pitiful in my eyes, and he's already pitiful enough in his own eyes), but he believes I favor the Monster because he's my birth child. Carla and April believe it, too, somewhere in themselves.

I won't deny that it probably mattered once, but not the way they think it matters. And there are many other things that have mattered much, much more.

I tell them what I always tell them, "I love all my children the same."

Petey nods and kisses me. April, too. They're patronizing me then, and patronizing themselves. But I can't undo it.

You never hear a child compelled to declare, "I love my parents and siblings equally."

Favorites are just . . . what? Unconsciousness?

But what's that anymore? Every day of the week you can watch cartoons with perfectly constructed Doctor Freud dreams put into them. How do you dream after taking in a few thousand of those?

———

Of course the Monster was manufacturing in my basement, and dealing, too. Of course, the fire started there. It could have. Of course.

THIS MIGHT BE a student's apartment, given the few bits of furniture we could scare up on short notice, and the general cheapness. I could have afforded more and better, despite Petey's insinuations to the contrary. But the wide empty walls and the clean shabbiness seemed, at first meeting, more hopeful than desperate. They still do. There's not much here to remind anyone. It's a temporary place not ashamed of itself for that. Most of the tenants of our little complex seem to be young women with children, fogies, or lonely middle-aged men who obviously eat too many microwave starches. I know three of the tenants by first name only, Shelby next door and her baby, Alana, and semi-blind Rubin. And there's also a fellow I call Stretch-pants Man who bounds into his sedan loaded with carpet samples at seven a.m. and returns at seven p.m. He waves to me if I can conjure an excuse to stick my head out the door.

I choose to see beginnings here (for myself most of all), though of course it's really just a bunch of ongoings.

I've been living here forty-four days (it's April 14th), and I've been writing now and then on Petey's old computer, to you, for a little while less than that.

Two months ago, I was living above the Monster and Cane Toad . . . and now, I'm here . . . and not here . . . at least, not all the way here yet.

Petey calls it change for the better. Ollie says difficult good fortune.

I have a daily schedule: Wake up (Good). Drink orange juice and eat a banana and check the action in the cornfield across Pleasant Hill Road. Wave at Stretch-pants Man. Browse the headlines on CNN. Maybe listen to a little NPR. Then down for a walk along Blue Jay Trail with April or Ollie or Petey or on my own. Then afterward, if I'm alone, one half a cigarette. (It's at this point I first started saying things out loud, not quite to myself, and then wept . . . and then started bawling outright through my stupid tight jaws . . . and began scratching on a pad of paper and, finally, switched on the computer.) Lunch is often out some-where, even if it's alone at the Hy-Vee deli. At least once a week, I also try to get together with my old high school pal Miriam, for lunch or a happy hour cocktail or golf. (Ray's game, actually. I learned to play out of duty to his business, but I still like to make a good shot, and it's wonderful to be outdoors, especially in the fall.) I also have my Sierra Club work, too, which I can be quite lazy about, and now there is Kate's anti-war committee rounding me up for events.

Sometimes, lately, I take a drive.

Then dinner at Petey's or April's. Or Ollie for dinner or a movie or maybe bed here or at his place.

Or dinner alone.

Amid all this, there's a good deal of staring and moping, and reading and phone chat, and trying to avoid the urge to nap by chasing after the basic chores. (I'm constantly surprised not to have the Monster downstairs, not to even have a downstairs to worry about anymore.)

I don't think a single one of the forty-four days here has actually transpired remotely like this, but you get the idea.

Even apartment complexes like this one (named Fox Trot or Vale Hollow or Hollow Eyes, or whatever) hardly existed in your time. I call it yours, though it was my time, too. Death somehow gives you the stronger claim on it.

I guess I started writing because each day since I've gotten the peacemaker seems, sooner or later, like a ghost . . . and also hasn't. I realize now the days have done this before in my life. I must be forgetting them less well now.

You're always twenty-seven, though it seems I sometimes try to imagine you older. Not as old as I am now, not that. It's just an empty wonder that can hurt and help me give up some power.

I don't really want you any more experienced than you are. You judge too much as it is, like a kid.

Mostly, I've wanted to keep you just as angry and stupidly hopeless as you were, wrapped up in your talent and your hatred of home. I have to keep you beautiful and troubled. I have to be justified, you bastard. I'm still here. It does no good to say I'm sorry.

You were exotic, so I'm guilty. You loved that. I loved it, too. How you could charm a woman like me, the drugstore owner's daughter who'd grown up beside Union Park in Des Moines, Iowa. It didn't take much, since so much was forbidden.

Still is, I can hear you say.

That's why we were there. To be so scared.

Okay, laugh. We can do that now, at least I imagine we could, smarter somehow. The world might find it quaint, too. I hope it would.

But I needed to know something no one near Union Park would know, something my mother certainly wouldn't know, even if she might secretly approve. That's all I wanted from you at first. Awful and small, isn't it? Just what I am. What we are. Right next to cliché. But it's no lie.

From the moment I saw you, your talk swelled me, so funny, whispering over your shoulder at that terrible poetry reading. I never understood poetry readings anyway.

I could hardly believe we were leaving the bookstore for a drink, a place you said we could all go. That's how you said it. How many of us. Six? I'd cajoled Marty, who'd been waitressing at Sally's Good Food about as long as I had, six months maybe, to come to the reading with me. I didn't have the courage to go on my own. Marty was an inspiration. She was five or six years older than I. Loud. Very independent, it seemed. We were going out often at the time, to the beach or downtown. She knew places. We'd even talked of renting an apartment together, until she'd tried to get me into bed. (We'd laughed that one off, horribly. I don't know now why I didn't try her, since I was looking for adventure.) She drank too much and loved sudden parties, but she was having none of this kind of getting picked up. Goodbye, Marty, you believe you understand what you're missing!

Funny, I don't actually remember that night in the far booth at Billie's Underpass. All the nights at Billie's are like one now, very pink in beer sign light. Except I remember your nervousness, just a twitch, and how you worked to make sure you were sitting opposite me. And your elbows, gray and dry like elephant eyes.

It was only afterward I realized how fully words could storm like flocks from you. Silver wings. Passion like that is attractive. I'd heard people argue about sports and politics, even literature, but never about photography. Not as though it were everything. That's how it was for you, wasn't it? Each thing could be everything.

Your tiny place on Eugenie, above the dry cleaner's that never seemed to be open. Your darkroom in the closet.

Whoops, it's Petey at the door. Must go.

YESTERDAY KATE PARKED us in the driveway of what used to be the house, just at the sidewalk, as though we might be pulling in only to turn around. I didn't want Petey to accompany me (he grumbles about the insurance company, which still hasn't settled), and I didn't want to go alone. The day I was released from the hospital, I made him drive me past it on the way to April's place. I felt about as wrecked as it looked, which may be why I wasn't shocked. My house was a charred and jagged box open to the snow just starting, and the snow fell through all that night.

Of course, I was thankful no one had been hurt, maybe even Cane Toad. I was grateful, too, that Ollie hadn't left me in the ordeal. And I was glad Ray wasn't alive to stand there with his fists on his hips and stare at the wreck like some moral failing of mine he'd try to be patient with. (He wouldn't have been conscious of it that way. It would have been too much.) In difficult times Ray grew very still, like a farmer at an auction already one bid over his limit and mulling a second. He liked to believe in me. It was exhausting but a sure gift I could offer him. Probably the only one.

He would have rebuilt, of course. But if he were still alive, the Monster and Cane Toad wouldn't have been living there in the first place, and maybe Kate and I wouldn't have ended up poking around those square, shiny ashes.

The air pulsed, a slight turn, and sent us whiffs from the char. And the interior seemed blacker in the sunlight. We couldn't draw close enough in most places to really get a good look. But once we walked around back, we could look through the kitchen windows and see where the middle of the house had collapsed in a heap onto the basement. It had been a fast, hot blaze, no doubt. Kate spotted the standing mirror (actually just part of the frame now, well scorched) in the far, north bedroom and started crying. That had been her and her sister Kelli's room when they lived with us, years ago.

"I used to spin around in front of it and pretend I was Paula Abdul on stage at Vet's Auditorium, remember?" She laughed in her tears, "Oh, Granna . . ."

I hugged her. This had been her house, too, her only steady house. The mirror had been my mother's. It had stood in my parents' room until her death. I remember her sitting in front of it one afternoon when I was about ten, trying to sketch herself smoking a cigarette.

Petey and April and Kate salvaged what they could from the ruins. There are probably other things that might be findable, a few small items underneath. But I don't know how anyone could get to them.

Barbara Jenner came over from across the street. (You only get about six minutes alone with your disaster before someone appears bearing their sympathies and questions.)

Barbara has always been personable, and she was again, "If there's anything I can do, please just say so." She took my hands in hers. I squeezed back and answered, "You've always been so kind. Don't worry about me, everything happens for a reason, it will all work out for the best." Over the years, she must have served a thousand weekends of dog dinners to the kids' pets while we were all at Panorama. She never seemed to go away herself. I guess I hadn't noticed that before now.

Though she didn't mention it, I'm sure she's wondering when we're going to bulldoze the thing.

At first, Petey spoke of rebuilding, to please me, I think. Since I'm not so sure about that prospect, or most any other, he's since stopped. He mentions selling the lot and buying a condo, though he knows I have a few debts, some pretty large credit cards from various cash advances to the Monster. He thinks he understands my assets. I've let him handle most of it lately. Why not?

Barbara peered into the wreckage with us. I think she'd been wanting to do that since the fire. I can't imagine her prowling around there on her own. She's been widowed for five years or more, and she must have watched all that was happening with the Monster and the cretins—and she certainly saw how the place was beginning to tatter at the edges since I was caring less and less what people thought as long as they kept a suitable distance.

Surely all those years with Ray I must have appeared as timid as Barbara seemed to me sticking her head in that knocked-out window. I was timid. I didn't feel timid, but then people rarely feel selfish, either.

It was clear to me we had to leave before I really started taking in any more of the reality. I lied and told Barbara I was staying at

April's and would be in touch. We hugged goodbye, as though I had a reason to come back there again.

———

Sometimes dying seems such an ordinary thing. It happens constantly, and so it is ordinary. But I mean it seems untroubling and about as burdensome as a carpool you have to meet. I almost want it to hurry up. I wanted that with my mother. She fought so hard against her sickness (and so successfully for almost five years) that I wanted her, in her worst moments (mine?), to get on with it. Awful to say, but I had an eagerness to see myself at her funeral, to try myself out as motherless. Maybe I thought I would have her and me settled, finally. (I could do all the talking for once?) Or maybe I thought I would then be verifiably like other people. I knew life was going on. My kids were marking their heights ever higher on the linen closet doorjamb.

I'M OLDER BY two years than my father (he died in 1971). I'm almost forty more than you. I wish I could sit you two down, one on each side of me, and have you tell me what you see. You couldn't grasp how long living can be, not really. And I can never be certain how short. That's the problem with dying young. Your survivors excuse your youth, finally, and make more sense of it than it ever had. We rack up the rationalizations, too. We undergo more, or think we do, encountering some of all those chances we come to believe you missed. That assurance comforts us, you missing so much that's lovely if we're lucky.

Funny, I think of him most often in his late forties, about the time I graduated from high school and went to college. I'd work Tuesday evenings and Saturdays at the drugstore behind the soda fountain. He's still there in the cubbyhole of the pharmacy, a toothpick in the corner of his mouth, figuring receipts. I suppose I'd ask him, if he were here like that, what most disappoints him about his life. I'd ask him because, for starters, he never got to finish his pharmacy degree and had to hire druggists for his business. My mother said she started calling him "Glee" not long after they met because he sang to himself and often whistled, and it exasperated her, that cheerfulness. She called him that to the end, only her. He placated her so clumsily she couldn't circumvent it. He even read the Bible in secret, back in the pharmacy. He'd hide it when I came into work with a great, nervous slamming shut of a drawer. I suppose he thought I'd snitch to Mother about it. She despised what she called "that pasty Christian hypocrisy."

I wonder how tuneful he would have been about you, either way.

I imagine him offering up something like: "Well . . . of course, but isn't self-slaughter a mortal sin?"

When I came back from Chicago, running from you, from us, he sized up my silence as significant. But he let me go about my problems on my own. I could have asked for help, of course, and gotten it. But I couldn't really have asked.

I was going to begin this entry by talking about how different you can be from yourself, even as you feel you're more or less who you've always been, no matter how often you've tried to bust out of your mold. You flip through a stack of snapshots of yourself and meet an exuberant tyke, or a career girl, or a coward. How many other people are in those other people grinning there with you?

Carla's right that I'm a liar. You were right to push me to become a painter, if that's what I wanted to do, figuring I never would. Ray was right to see I was no natural mother, that I would need shaming and more if we were to keep Petey and April under our roof after Phil dumped them.

"They're your family," Ray said.

I wanted to say, "I don't care. I didn't have them. They're not my choice. Their parents are drunks and who knows what else. We don't know them. We'll have two kids in second grade, for Chrissakes!"

"They need a place," he said, as if that were all there was to it.

I wanted to say but didn't, "You know, I'm overwhelmed with the kids already. I need to get out of the house. I need time to myself. What about me?"

"Who else in the family can take them in?" Ray asked. "Your parents, with your father sick?" So moral, Ray. So disgustingly good.

I wanted to say, "I'm thirty-three years old. This isn't fair!"

Why didn't I speak up? It was 1970, feminism and all. It's not as though I hadn't asserted myself before.

Instead, I brooded. I sank somewhere below politeness and covered myself up with inertia. You know how I let that silence in and it takes over. I can't find a way to oust it without a shock.

Or maybe you don't understand this about me? Maybe it became part of me afterward.

Ray and I had just bought the big split-level. He was in his mid-forties, and I think he still flirted with the idea of us having one more child.

"Can you live with yourself, really," he said, "if we let those children go to the state?"

I wonder if he would have argued so eagerly for them at, say, thirty?

I've had a lot of time without him here to contradict me (which is partly why I've gotten into trouble with the Monster, of course). Ray would be surprised at me (I'm older than he now, too), and he'd pretend he wasn't surprised.

My parents were grateful we took Petey and April, of course. They must have feared they would be stuck with them. It's true, my father was already feeble. (His heart.) He died the next year.

So I was allowed to feel like a good daughter to him in that brief beforehand.

Carla was only five when Petey and April moved in, and suddenly fourth in line instead of second. Would she be less angry at me now if she'd remained second?

Would she have changed her name?

The truth is you can end up as the near opposite of yourself over and over.

You and I were always fretting that we hadn't lived.

I've never "lived."

Who actually does?

I wish I could say I hate to pull rank on you here, but I don't. You never tested out this difficulty, I'm afraid, because it requires that you wander through a good many years. You have to pass the point where you still believe you can become nearly anything. That's a lamentable position in life, but I'm not lamenting it now. After all, some insight attaches itself, like a virus. I don't think I'll live long enough for it to mature, however.

More than anything, I've feared I haven't loved.

Yes. That old trouble.

We want to be inspired. We want to be imaginative and amazing. But we're only as good as we practice being.

It's somehow unsavory to hear old people talk about problems with their parents. Aren't they supposed to have outgrown that (or grown resigned, if still cognizant of the matter at all)? Therapy is for the future. How much pain and enlightenment and self-knowledge do you need at the end? Is it a matter of being near enough the end, or far enough, too far maybe, from the start?

At the museum shop today I saw a refrigerator magnet with a quote from Eleanor Roosevelt (they're making her into a sage): "Every day do something that scares you."

I bought it.

Writing here is getting to be a habit.

NIGHT NUMBER EIGHT at Ollie's.

Who am I kidding, with him sidesaddle between these legs?

Early on, I "confessed" to him that I was sixty. I can pass for it. I don't have that deadly widening part in my hair just yet, and the hair itself is still dark enough naturally that the dye job doesn't look too phony. I can still dress as though I shop for the latest within reason, thanks mainly to Miriam, and Kate.

I don't think he believes me. I don't dare think it. His taste has to be . . . unconventional. Right? We go easy on the past, he and I, not so eager to use it up in swapping stories, I think, as we might have been had we met years ago. I never thought I could use up the past until now. And I don't want mine to pile up, especially the repeated stories.

But he told me that he used to seek out fat women, when he had lovers at all, because they were often grateful.

"That was a long time ago," he said, as though he were some heavy voice-over on the history channel.

I wonder how much gratitude I'm supposed to have now. I've got plenty, believe me. I never let myself get big, even with my decent frontage.

Young women can go out anywhere now with wet hair. My generation couldn't. I guess that's another one I missed. I spend too much energy noticing that kind of thing.

Last night, as we lay there, he moving in me just a little now and then (some Tantric trick he was trying out, and I humored him, why not?), he mentioned his cabin in the Upper Peninsula of Michigan. "A family heirloom," he said, "with no more family."

He wants us to go there. So he said.

I'm amazed how firm his body is, even though he's flabby by any modest standard. The luxury of being a man. I'm amazed all the time, in little bursts.

We have to make love mostly in the dark. That's my fault.

I left Ollie's before dawn. I didn't want another blue gown morning.

Driving home in the pearly light. That was a first for me. No wonder all the boys write poems about traipsing home from the boudoirs at sunrise. You own everything for a little while, with your lips rubbed so much the kissing still seems underway. It made me feel close to Ray just after we'd met, when he'd leave my apartment on Walnut and go right to work at the store.

I've never tried writing a poem. It's not me. I've kept diaries a little, after you and then for awhile after Ray died. Spiral notebooks. I burned each one. There came a day when it hurt just to see it on the table. It seemed to want something I don't know.

Some people think burning a diary is a crime. I hoped it would be a freeing act. I think I liked the pain.

On the way here, I stopped in at Dunkin Donuts and ordered two apple fritters and a tall coffee. I didn't want to get home too fast.

I'm so tired I feel like running out and hugging Stretch-pants Man (he's leaving right now). I should go to sleep. But no way.

OLLIE: Why don't we go up to the woods for awhile?

JILL: And what would we do there?

OLLIE: We'd make a little lazy household. Pick some wildflowers. Why not?

JILL: That's very gallant.

OLLIE (a little exasperated, and rightfully so): Please, don't try to pull rank on me.

JILL (looking at him, a foolish expression): What about April, Petey, the kids?

OLLIE: They seem fine to me.

JILL (excited but nervous and wary): What about your work?

OLLIE: I can work anywhere there's a phone line.

JILL: Are you crazy?

OLLIE: Of course. Aren't you?

JILL: It's just that—

OLLIE: Let's give it a whirl. It'll be summer soon enough. Hey, we'll fish. What's really keeping you here, anyway?

JILL (thinking of the Monster but trying not to show it): Well . . .

OLLIE (sighing and turning away to pour himself more coffee): That's not my business.

JILL (wanting to ask him who Laura Aussoway is): I've already been a burden to you.

OLLIE: When are you going to give that one up?

JILL (laughing and pulling out a cigarette to distract herself from herself): You terrify me, you know.

OLLIE: Stop hiding, my sweet.

JILL: Got a match?

O WHO SHOULD spot me in the Hy-Vee parking lot today but Cane Toad and two of the cretins. They were leaning on the fenders of a pickup. I was coming out with groceries, just a couple of bags in the cart, and I hurried to my car, trying not to seem like I was hurrying. Cane Toad raced over as I opened the trunk.

"How are you, Mrs. Lundgrove?" he asked. That voice. So polite. As though he might whack you in the head with a hammer any second.

"I'm quite well," I said. "Thank you."

I didn't exactly make eye contact. He grabbed the last grocery bag as though he were helping. But he really just wanted to keep it from me.

"I'm sorry to hear about your house, the fire and all," he said, as though he hadn't been around there for months on end, as though he could be sorry about anything.

I had to look at him, and he smiled. A shambles, really. Something surprisingly shy about him in the sunlight, like a cracked windowpane.

God, what his mother must be . . .

"Thank you," I said. I tried to take the bag, but he held it a little longer. "I'm just glad no one was hurt," I said.

I thought he might mention the Monster then. Instead, he just watched me trying not to seem like I was running off. I also thought I might ask him how the Monster is doing. But who knows what relations they have, if any, now that the Monster isn't good for a crash pad. It would queer my soul, him ever thinking he had something I could want.

"Well, goodbye," I said and slammed the trunk and scooted into the driver's seat. A couple were loading their SUV nearby, and a clerk was gathering shopping carts. It occurred to me that it might be safer to stay put than drive off, except I might appear to need assistance of some sort, and this might attract rather than repel the cretins.

This store is miles from the old neighborhood but not all that far from the apartment. April, Petey, Miriam, Ollie, and Kate are the only ones who know where I live at present. April won't speak to the Monster and leaves the room when he enters. Kate pities him, but she's my girl.

I pulled out and headed for the ring road, wary. A few minutes later, there was Cane Toad at the wheel of the pickup, cretins at his right hand, with about four cars between us.

My heart was a bunch of leaping slivers, I was so scared.

No way I would take the exit to the apartment, so I kept going. I drove halfway across town, out past the airport exit, before he finally flew right up into my mirror and honked about ten times and then blasted past, grinning, the goon.

———

When I think of Cane Toad's mother, I want to believe she must be like that nutty woman in the news last fall who lay down (or passed out?) on the couch and slept while her pet raccoon gnawed off her screaming infant's nose and lips. Milk on the infant's lips was the attraction.

THEY WEREN'T ALL bad, the '70s. I can call up summer memories, but autumn ones come first, without effort. The ones that need me the most? (You'd laugh at that one. Ray would, too. But he'd love me for it, confused.)

The smell of burning leaves at Panorama. And the thump, thump, thump of the Monster and Petey shooting baskets all afternoon. That's my sound for the boys together.

Terribly routine. That was one of the things I liked about that time.

We played double-deck pinochle with Miriam and Al, who often came out for the weekends.

Ray cleaned bullheads the kids caught. He might tongue the inside of his bottom lip.

"Are you getting a cold sore?" I'd ask.

"Boy, are we married," he'd say, sarcastically if you wanted to hear it that way.

Moonlight. How many nights could it have been, really?

One Labor Day weekend, 1973, Ray and I woke up and sneaked down to the shore very, very late, the kids asleep, and sat with the glitter on the water. Then we went in, slipping off the end of the dock.

We weren't talking much at the time and somehow not suffering anymore for not talking. What would we have said? (Since his death, I've often thought I missed many chances there.)

Funny, I could speak to Ray in those days by letting him overhear me chat with his sister, or my mother, on the phone. I'd say something and look at him, and he'd grin or make a face. Sometimes I'd call them just to bring him near me. Too often it was the only way. Not that I praised him. He told me once he liked the glow in my voice. I think of those cats that will never sit in a lap but will loll by the hour beside human conversation. What do they hear, those cats? I think Ray was just glad to find me free of my Drears.

You knew me when I didn't say things under my breath. I'm fond of the notion that I learned to lie with Ray, but that's not so, exactly.

We were in that era of us when you realize that you can still have your thoughts and you don't have to fight for them. You don't have to fight to have them, against your parents or children or your husband.

Part of the gift of the routine is in disappearing. You can vanish for a few years, and then one day you're back.

Like the morning you touch the bathroom mirror and realize: It's in this one I will age.

Ray grew wittier as he grew sadder, though that was later. I can't remember a single humorous thing he said that could be repeated without a huge story behind it. Now it's just a chime in my head.

I slipped into Ray's arms in the water because the night was warm and beautiful and he'd begged me, and I realized my chance, for once, just as I'd begun to realize that he and my friend Miriam had been trying to have an affair. (I'd found the condoms in his briefcase. We didn't use them, he said he hated them.) Though I can't be sure, I'm surmising they'd rendez-voused only once or twice at that point. Earlier in the evening, they'd been unusually fidgety over cards, and she got the most melodramatic headache to send her and Al back to town. And we wouldn't see them alone again for almost two years.

Long before this, I would come at Ray sometimes, after weeks apart, after centuries of my Drears, it seemed. And anything could discourage me. That's what takes the effort—not to be discouraged after you've put yourself out there in pursuit of something that used to come to you so easily you hardly noticed except to fend it off. I could turn the bedroom light down suddenly, and a few minutes later he could flick on the overhead and leap up to put his eyeglasses on the dresser, so they'd be out of whatever harm's way he'd imagined. Or he couldn't let his shirt fall to the floor, as I wanted it to, desperately, after unbuttoning it, but would hang it on the doorknob, just so—and I would half dry up right away. I'd pause then in that light, that prudent light, ready to race from the room. Everything was lost, it seemed. Then he'd switch off the lamp, and I'd dip deep, stretch across the bed, snake toward him, to give myself time to recover from the sense that we were futile. Why not admit it? Occasionally I'd imagine the Jenners' oldest son, Ted, who was graduating from Iowa State. He used to wash his car in the front yard, across from our picture window. A handsome boy with good legs. The pillow went over my face because I didn't want Ray to see me. He thought I didn't want to see him.

And yet we found our way sometimes. The way the hands move in sleep, gently to the nape, along the hip. They're grateful hands, they're hands relieved they're not alone, they're relieved they don't have to say anything about how they got to be that way.

A COUPLE DAYS AFTER my encounter with Cane Toad, Petey came by for a sandwich. I didn't mention what happened. Petey's frustrated about the house insurance, which is still "in process" . . . and about Jane. The latter's an always, though he won't admit it. She's finagling for a mini-SUV she saw in a magazine, even as he's worrying himself toward an early college tuition program for his kids. Jane, he says, insists the kids should choose their own schools when the time comes. Perfect strategy for her ends . . . and typical.

"The reality is that Cane Toad should be in jail. I know he's behind the fire," Petey grumbled. "But what good would putting him there do us?"

Petey believes he'd like to see the Monster in jail, too, but, like the pain of Jane, he'll never say so.

I considered mentioning Ollie's proposal about going to Michigan. Petey needs to hear it pretty soon. Ollie's idea is better than my silly and vain presumption that he was thinking of marriage. (I must be thinking of marriage, though when have I thought of marriage?) Ollie's plan leaves us on vacation but with some dangerous and, I suppose, wonderful frontier. He's figured out that much fun. And that much of me, maybe.

Who am I kidding? I'm lazy. I've always liked myself.

Petey still believes I'll give the insurance money to the Monster, though he hasn't shouted that one at me in awhile. Of course, he hasn't had cause.

I have to convince him that Ollie isn't taking the Monster's place at the purse.

Here I think of Miriam with her twins. They're between Petey and the Monster in age. So long ago, we'd sit over coffee, Miriam and I, and she'd tell me she'd hug one for getting a good math score at school, but then the other would have to have a hug and would be angry if she couldn't give it.

"You're the sun," Miriam would say, "and they revolve around you. You have to recognize that."

I suppose many don't, or they don't really want to be gods, or don't have the stamina or the need for it. And so they try to elude it, to gain themselves some . . . what? Privacy? And so they hurt those eager for their light and pull.

CARLA CALLED TODAY.

I haven't told her about Ollie, but she's surely apprised since she heard about my going to the anti-war protest. I didn't ask her about changing her name.

She said she wanted to know how I'm doing.

"Fine, dear," I said. I don't know where to begin.

I can see her expression at my reply, that single blink of the eye like the number flipping on the digital clock in the night. The anger blink.

She couldn't take my truth. I suppose I can't take hers.

When someone dies, along with everything else you lose a way of talking and listening.

Maybe that's why we talk to phantoms.

Ray used to shout me down, that's what they did in his family, and because he knew I would shout him down if he didn't. I decided I might be more interesting, at least to myself, if I let that shouting go. It took me twenty years, by increments. Learning to shut up and not seem to be shutting up. I think of it now that this place is so silent.

They say it's good to express yourself, but I don't think my shouting got me one wish. A lot of old dead leaves crackled in my mouth when I shouted at Ray the same thing for the five-hundredth time.

Now I'm criticized for being silent, for being compliant. Carla must surely realize I can hear her at the other end of the line, turning the pages of a magazine, opening her mail.

Here's how funny I can get. What if Carla has changed her name to Laura Aussoway? What if she's been corresponding with Ollie all this time? What if she arranged for Ollie and me to meet? What would she be telling Ollie about me now?

———

Kate and I walked two miles on Blue Jay Trail. She actually wanted to talk with me about her boyfriend, Stephen. He's older, by five years, it turns out. I guessed as much when she brought him around for a quick viewing at April's Easter dinner. Kate surprises me with her need. I think she's grown up, and then she asks me if he'll care she's not a virgin. The question was sidelong but clear.

Stephen is not exactly religious, Kate said, but spiritual. That must be an attraction, since he's plain butter as far as looks go, and you can see that plainer is on the way, once those curls just starting to recede are finally gone. He's after something he believes. And the age difference . . . well, that was a draw for me with you. With Ray, too. Though it turns out that so many of our friends were Ray's first, and now they're truly aged and rickety.

"He's very intense," Kate said. "He's the one who got the anti-war committee started . . . He's always writing. And reading this mystical philosophy."

I implied that a man wouldn't care about a woman's virginity, if he cared about her.

That was surely my duty as her grandmother.

She and Stephen (never Steve) share the enchantment of changing the world. Lucky them. You have to hope it's enough.

So I endorsed as much as possible. Where else is Kate likely to go, if she doesn't start here? How else will she find out how little she knows? I doubt she speaks to her mother about her life. Sheila's managed to keep a job all these years, with that cleaning service, and has finally stopped trying to dress like a teenager. But mostly Kate and Kelli have had to teach themselves what to think. And Kelli is so attached to her mother, so doomed to Sheila's soap opera, Kate has been walking my way for a long time. Maybe she's walking elsewhere now. Of course.

I've got to get over trying to save her, especially since I don't have a genuine clue what I'd be saving her for.

Kate didn't mention her father, and I didn't bring him up, though I admit I wonder about him. I assume she's had some contact.

Blue Jay Trail is greening up furiously, like a halo around that girl. I told her about Ollie. I wanted her to understand that I still . . . still what?

The expression on her face. There's no dogwood as blossoming. And I'm a little ashamed to be so proud.

I asked her not to mention Ollie and Michigan to anyone, though I guess she'll have a tough time keeping that pony in her pocket.

CARLA IS JEALOUS of me because she believes I've always arranged things just the way I want them. I'm ruthless, she thinks. Carla would like to arrange things for herself but doesn't know how. Oh, she's accomplished. She's made it. She's an attorney, with plenty of public interest work on the side to soothe her conscience. But that's not the thing she wants. She wants what she thinks I have, what I've had.

This endless war on TV . . . And now they're taking Baghdad. And all these appeals on the internet for money to aid political prisoners.

It's just another start when you try to think of the eyes put out and the fingers withered by fire. Real people there.

You. Me. Carla. Everyone.

I'm trying to understand.

Every day, sooner or later, my peacemaker pinches a little. When I pick up the phone a certain way, or maybe when I roll onto my left side in bed, I'm reminded. And I try to feel the wires there correcting my heart, when I can bear to think about it. But there's nothing to feel, except in the shower, when I run soap over that tight skin.

On one of those dumb talk shows a while ago (I think it was

Montel) some woman's daughter wanted to reconcile the past for her mother. So she set up this meeting, on national TV, with her mother and the fiancé who'd jilted her mother after he found out he'd been drafted and was being sent to Vietnam. So now this middle-aged man in bifocals saunters out onto the stage and explains to her mother that he ran away from their engagement because he couldn't be sure he'd come back alive from the war, and by the time he found out he wasn't going to Vietnam, he'd "already dug himself into such a rut" he couldn't get out.

Then he apologizes.

Then her mother says let's dance.

And they do.

Horrible little puppets.

And, yes, the whole thing cut me up with chuckles and then a few thick tears I swear almost seemed to stink.

Montel appeared afterward to inform us, with a straight face, that this meeting took place some months before and the couple has since discovered, after twenty-five years apart, they are different people, and so they are taking a break from each other, not really going into new or old relationships just yet, since they're both recently divorced.

Why am I wasting my energy on this?

I THINK YOU WANTED each moment to be like a party you hated to leave but you know you must because there are better things ahead—this is only one glass of wine, and now there will be a film and after that a glittering conversation by the pool and after that a drive into the mountains and then a nightcap and then fucking madly and then the morning, the chance for the gorgeous light on the table and the orange in the juice and then more.

You taught me to hate the ordinary, which is what I was, what I am.

You said, "Right now should always be a heartbreak of going," and fed me a spoonful of spumoni, there on the rusty fire escape.

"Ordinary life," you declared, "is a lie."

You were so interested in lies. Children are.

W E GIVE BIRTH, and we're birthed. So something is of us. We are of something.

Ray went through me into our children. Or he went through me and took some of me into our children.

But here I am. Still just me.

Am I going to lie beside Ray in death?

How often I haven't really thought of that.

We only knew each other as life.

Often I remember us lying in bed, smoking a cigarette. I don't think we were imitating the movies, though it might look like that now. Ray's legs seem so long and slim . . . and the fan whirring in the window, the blades like a ghostly disk in the glow of the streetlight. Wonderful.

I woke up with Ollie today (no more counting the nights), but first I rose and rose and rose through fear that was like a cold gel. It pressed on my chest. It was like a sticky bubble I was making on the surface of sleep as I pressed to break through.

I finally let myself tell Ollie about it, and felt better, after some coffee.

NEXT WEEK MIRIAM is taking another of her eco-tours, this one to Costa Rica. Her rouged cheeks and drawstring hat, that big floppy-dop—Miriam and the howler monkeys, with her young guide. That's how she gets close to men, since Al's gone. She follows her cane and wins her hireling with her gusto, clambering through the rainforest somewhere, on the path, of course, and then asking him to boost her up a couple of steps, his hands on her hips.

It's a way to be touched, if you need it. Better than the beauty parlor, or the manicurist. She tried to get me to go with her a couple of years back. I didn't dare leave the Monster under my roof. But, really, I was scared enough without marching off like that. I remember Ted Robinson, at the store, had tried to romance me after Ray died. He was taller than Ray . . . and that put me off. Anything would have put me off, poor man. He'd been a top salesman for Ray. And Ray used to claim that we owed the place at Panorama to Ted, all his record-breaking. Ted probably hoped I grasped that accomplishment when he called me the first time. He'd looked at me over the years, and I'd enjoyed it. Who wouldn't, though he ogled nearly everyone. I didn't imagine any follow-up in candlelight. Ted *was* a salesman, all those jokes, and that white Lincoln. Funny, I think of him sometimes when I see Stretch-pants Man, though Ted was in better shape. His fingernails, not a single wayward cuticle. His wife had left him several years before, and he'd never gotten over it. He had no one to dominate as he had Alice, I think. No one to apologize to. He wanted to be gracious, but I think he used most of that capacity in closing deals on disc harrows.

We never said a word about Ray or Alice. We never got that far. Ray had been dead two years. I'd resolved not to talk of him as though he were alive . . . and no reminiscing. I was so miserable at being relieved of his illness. It seemed a proof of how ungrateful I'd been.

Miriam and I don't speak often of Ray and Al, and then only to laugh at their slightest foibles, as though they were meeting us after lunch. Maybe we've said too little for too long.

Of course, I'd figured out she and Ray were trysting. That was 1973. Bringing Petey and April into the house had gone more awry than Ray had imagined it could. And my father had died a couple of years before—just smiled at dinner and collapsed. I should have been ready but wasn't. We should all be ready. So I'd sumped around, justifiably, for awhile.

When Petey and April had arrived it seemed to me there must be an impending holiday . . . or maybe someone must be visiting us on vacation . . . since these kids, a nephew and niece I'd just met, were here in the house, trying to play with my children. But the vacation never ended. No other adults showed up. Instead, I put out four bowls of Cheerios instead of two, every morning.

We all just kept meeting.

Petey and April needed their mother every time I appeared. Eventually, that made me grow up again. Petey would follow me around the basement while I sorted laundry. I tried to coax him into chatting about his mother, if he'd like to. (The adoption counselor suggested we should welcome her as a subject.) But Petey would shrug and draw his hot rods and airplanes. He claims not to have many memories of her—even now, when he has no reason to butter me up as the one and only.

After he'd decided he would maybe stay with us (eight years old!) he never let me or April out of sight for long. That lasted at least a year. It wore April out more quickly than it did me. Not to mention Monte and Carla.

No matter what problems he faces with family, Petey likes to declare, "You don't revise your expectations of your children."

I suppose he also means he never stopped hoping for Ray and me.

Ray and I had figured out a sweet enough start with Carla and Monte. I've always believed that. We were a long way from the point when you swear you have nothing more to say to each other because you don't really say anything different to yourself.

But then, suddenly, that wasn't good enough anymore.

Of course, I could imagine Ray on top of Miriam at the Travelodge. These things occur to you when you don't want to witness yourself in your life. Like waking up again and here you are.

It's not like I hadn't done anything wrong myself.

Ray was a lousy concealer. I sensed he was hurting guilty when he turned toward me one night in bed and kissed my shoulder lightly but very long, just once, and turned away.

I'd been extremely turned away from him myself . . . angry, I'll admit, for longer than either of us understood about what seemed like his sticking me with a clingy, jealous brood while he went out to meet adults at the office. Not that I wasn't heartbroken for the kids, for their being stuck with me and my attitudes. It was odd to feel suddenly so far from Ray, to feel justified and soothed and scared by the fresh distances. I wouldn't let the kids down, whatever that would mean. They were already having me, anyway. But I was already letting other parts (those they didn't claim) float away. It was aggressive, sure. Having most of your real resolutions made for you by others will do that.

Ray's kiss inspired thought. Then I collected evidence.

And maybe someone tries to help you to see what's happening behind you . . . for your own good, they think. Or maybe out of pride, or joyful meanness. Anyway, someone did step forward—Betsy Handlin. Her daughter worked as a ticket taker at Adventureland, next to a motel where Miriam and Ray met one time. She just happened to spy them going into a room. She mentioned it to Betsy, who, once she got started, desperately wanted to do my inferring for me.

It hadn't struck her that I might be anything but ruined by the news.

"You know, there's probably a good explanation for it," she said.

I vowed to myself she'd never hear it. She got nothing but cordiality from me.

But I can't be too hard on her anymore. After all, she did try to tell some truth. She died of cancer, too, back in the late '80s. She was in tremendous pain, and as a last-ditch effort, they put her into an experimental drug trial. She was so hopeful, since a few other patients had responded to the treatment. It didn't work for her. But then maybe she'd been one of those given the sugar water.

———

I'm back, after lying down for about twenty minutes of denying myself a nap.

That's what people do: they get up from a failed nap and say, about an old betrayal, you get past these things.

Because people do.

They have to.

There was a blue-handled knife that scared me like nothing inanimate ever has. I was washing it one evening, at the kitchen sink, along with a few other dishes. The kids were in bed. Ray was pouring himself a glass of beer. I saw my reflection in the window and looked away and felt, really felt, we all deserve better treatment than that.

My hands stopped, the knife there in the dish towel. Like it was being presented. I felt the knife was going to jump with my hand and stick Ray, more than once.

Ray had his back to me. He said something funny and sweet. I felt so sorry for him. Ashamed, shaken. I saw him falling to the floor, the astonished expression on his face, blood everywhere. God, I was awful.

What I mean is I realized right then I had to fix my love on him more than ever before.

It's too simple to think that moment should help me understand the way you could get sometimes. You frightened me so differently.

Not that it matters.

I folded the knife up in that dish towel, right then. I bagged it and slipped it into the trash, quickly, as though there was nothing strange about it.

Ray didn't notice he was just then allowed another chance to grow old.

I decided I couldn't let myself imagine that when he was with me he was thinking of Miriam or someone else. No more creeping up to that.

I calculate that Miriam and Ray lasted three months, at most. About ten years later Ray more or less admitted it had happened. Once, he wanted to be more specific, feeling quite contrite, I guess. But I waved it away before he could get started. I didn't want to have to explain how he didn't understand.

I've always wondered, though, if Al knew, and if he'd also been possessed by a blue knife.

THE MONSTER LEFT a message on my cell today: "Hey, Ma. Cane said he saw you at the grocery store. He said you look pretty good . . . I hope so . . . Well, I hope I can see you soon, sometime. I've been working a little, a remodel in Ankeny . . . Well, I love you. Give me a call sometime. Love you."

I listened to it once and almost erased it right away. That would have been a first. But, as you see, I've written it down.

I'm not ready for him, it's true.

I encountered Cane Toad a week ago, so I wonder why it's taken him so long to call . . . if they're still running together. Maybe he's getting my message. Do I have a message for him just yet?

That likelihood amounts to this: I drive past a new restaurant, say, and I want to go into it. I long to support it because suddenly I think it will fail if it doesn't have my support. I think of all who need me and how I've failed them (April, Monte, Ray, Kate). I think of the gifts I could give them, the favors I could do them . . . and soon, I'm panicking. They're all glaring at me like the man behind the counter of the restaurant I haven't yet entered—all those waiting for me, for whom I haven't done, don't know how to do.

The terrible thing about this gender is that a single gesture (sighing at the wrong moment) can undo you.

JILL: I don't think any of us really knows how to talk about the good times in our lives. We talk about conflict. Maybe that's to avoid silence? We do a lot out of habit, mostly . . .

OLLIE: You hauled me to that protest at the capitol.

JILL: So?

OLLIE: That was different, wasn't it? . . . It was very brave . . . I think.

JILL: I'm not brave.

OLLIE: What are you then?

JILL (nervous laughter): I'm a failed mom.

OLLIE (pause): I guess you have a point.

JILL (surprised, a little hurt): What?

OLLIE: Well, here you are, as you say, unable to acknowledge the good, especially the good you *have* done.

JILL: That's not what I meant.

OLLIE (pretending to be somewhere ahead of her): Really?

Ray and I used to talk about the kids as though we could extrapolate from their behavior what each would become. Carla seems a people person. I bet she'll go into politics. April loves animals. A vet? Look at Monte throw!

The sweetest kind of fear talk.

It's a sure twist. Like the day your daughter feels sick and sleeps all afternoon. But then arises refreshed, not ill at all. Except her legs ache. And you realize what it is. She's been growing.

Ray never expected any of them to come into the business,

though Carla worked several summers at the store. He was prouder of her than the rest, I think, prouder of her for going to law school. But he made sure they all had their chances. That was how he said it. Their chances. He was excellent that way.

Your child becomes you in some way you can't escape. That's how you come under the illusion you've done right, or wrong, by her.

I gave Monte his nickname by accident when he threw a frog from the car window on the way home from the lake. He'd been tormenting Carla with it, and I turned to pop him and perhaps negotiate. But out went the poor creature.

You little monster!

Ray laughed and wouldn't let it pass. He repeated it. Laughing and singing it out. Soon the other kids took it up and we all repeated it. Monte, too. Laughing. So it stuck. A joke that was finally no joke.

Suddenly, you can't name the favorite in this year's Kentucky Derby . . . or the biggest young TV stars. The price of a postcard stamp has risen two cents since you bought one last. This slipping begins much earlier, maybe in your late forties. It's familiar now but just as unfriendly.

How old was I when I decided to become like my father? At what age, really, did I discover he wasn't perfect (that he wasn't always nice and didn't love all the people at his church)? When did I first imagine my mother was working—so, so slightly— to turn me and Phil and Greta against him, only because she wanted us for herself?

She, who when I paid the Monster's bills after he and Sheila moved in with us, would ride me about it, claiming I was being selfish.

Was that actually Phil, my beautiful drunk-under-construction brother, who convinced me that marrying Terry Jenkins would be the most foolish endeavor? Leave Des Moines, Phil said, go off to New York, or Chicago, California . . . I did, didn't I?

M Y HOUSE-REMAINS WERE bulldozed today. Long overdue.

In the morning, Petey came over, accompanied by the
insurance representative with a few last questions . . . and
forms for me to sign. From Petey's manner in dealing with au-
thorities in this matter, I've surmised I'm supposed to be officially confused about the nature of the Monster's basement business and, thus, useless as a source of clues to the possible origins
of the fire. Since I'd been flatlining in the hospital at the time of
the blaze, I could shrug again today in good enough conscience
and offer another cup of coffee.

The weather, daggerly all April (now Armageddon-by-global-
warming, now frost at dawn on the back step) is coming around
to real hopefulness. Familiar sunlight right there on the cheek.

I declined Petey's invitation to witness them push the wreck
into a pile and shovel that into a dump truck. But Ollie drove
me over there this evening. The lot is scraped clean. The broken foundation surrounds a blackened, cracked basement floor.
The driveway leads to a slab where the garage stood. Petey had
them take the two sycamores that had shaded the window at the

kitchen sink. The whole place seems surprised, really, to be so naked, arranged like this for a beginning.

The house was worth twice what we'd paid for it. Imagine. We'd never really considered leaving it, even during the worst with the Monster. In one period of relative Monte and Sheila independence, Ray did suggest we sell and move permanently out to the lake, but I refused straightaway. His sister was wise (or lucky) enough to keep herself out there full-time. But she also craved talk—craves it still—and that means a banquet of listening. I could envision the dire code I'd be forced to impose on her: when the garage door is up, I'm ready for company; when it's down, I'd like privacy. Every day I'd have to choose which injustice I could endure.

I've lost two houses, now, at least. Ray left me with insurance money, and the business . . . and that should have sufficed, I'll admit. We sold the store when it became clear no one in the family wanted to take it over. Later, after I'd funded a couple of the Monster's larger failures, Petey insisted he would buy the lake place, to relieve me of the pressures of upkeep, and to keep it in the family. Though he didn't say it, he was afraid I was going through my money and didn't trust me to keep the Monster from eating up the lake house, too. He was trying to save everyone from what I'll admit looked like my approaching destitution, since I think he planned to put the purchase money in trust for me.

I told him that the place at Panorama was everyone's to use, and there was no need for such a financial shuffle.

But I was undependable, I can see that now. I probably could see it then.

At the time, Petey was mortgage-tight and didn't have access to kind financing, not that the purchase required a fortune. But this was ten years ago, and he simply hadn't advanced yet under Jane's career accelerator life-effect. And Carla and April wanted nothing to do with the plan. So he went into partnership with some "friend" from the dairy.

He's my son, and he can be convincing. And this was something I could do for him for a change. And the price was fair, as far as I could determine.

Of course, it went wrong. They bought the place, and rather than Petey buying out his partner in three years, as planned, the opposite happened. I don't understand the details of their agreement, but Petey could be compelled to sell and did. The boom of the '90s brought it on. Petey's partner had to dole out some profit to Petey to take complete control. But the land had become so valuable he bulldozed our little place, subdivided and put up three shoreline giants.

Goodbye, Panorama. Where the shirtless fat men race their speed boats, their breasts jiggling across the waves. . . .

JILL (trying it out): April and Howard have offered to build a cottage for me on their farm.

OLLIE: Oh, that might be interesting.

JILL: Howard is behind it.

OLLIE: Yeah?

JILL: After I'm gone, he can convert it into an outbuilding. A chicken coop, maybe.

OLLIE (stroking his chin): Practical . . . don't you think?

JILL (stroking her chin, in time): Practically heaven . . . for at least a week . . . the thing would have to be close to the other buildings, to serve its afterlife. I don't think I could afford it.

OLLIE: The living is free in the UP.

JILL (laughing): Is that what they say there?

OLLIE: That's what they say on Piper Lake.

JILL: Pied Piper?

OLLIE: Pie-eyed, maybe.

(LONG silence, passing scenery)

OLLIE: The house there can be winterized . . . But you don't have to think about that until—

JILL: Oll, I've known you six months—

OLLIE: I thought we already discussed that part . . . Hey, I'm just inviting you to go have sex with me there. It's not like I'm asking you to come up and do something life-changing, like fishing.

I'll sell the lot in town and its missing house. I'm glad to finally do it. There. I'm supposed to say that like I'm supposed to cry. I don't even know how to begin that project.

I drove and Ollie rode, out into the countryside, part of the way west toward Panorama. But then I turned around near Redfield, and we came back here. He's asleep down the hallway, in my bed . . . on his stomach, with a pillow underneath his belly to ward off waking with a backache.

Those miles you drive through . . . miles of nothing that hold a cracked robin's egg or a broken turtle shell.

SCROLL BACK OVER these pages, to see where I've been lately, and it's like trying to make out one real detail in a pretentious ladies' room mirror. Some designer (probably a man) who doesn't use such things as the mirror, at least not the way you want to use it, has insisted on a countertop so grand and wide you're miles from the face you're trying to fix. And the light's dim, glinty, pitched from too far above, and it mostly illuminates your body, anyway.

But I'm still flattered, which reminds me why I threw out my diaries before. Make them and break them, the same impulse.

Petey, I should register here, in the interest of bad lighting, hasn't forgotten how the lake place was lost. Always frontal and always safely unaccountable, Carla wouldn't let him forget it. And April has carried her silence on the matter to him.

It hurt to watch the surprise quarter him, again and again.

But the whole undertaking . . . To me, that surprise resembled the kind we've all witnessed whirling around so many people about this war, about all the terrible developments since those awful attacks on New York a couple of years ago . . . terrorists in turbans versus those in suits and ties. As though we've just now invented cruelty and must deal with the discovery of a miraculous power—instead of merely realizing we've always been on its payroll, head down, punching in, punching out.

Get the fix on—wham!—and we can all go back to worrying about car payments and how we can evade jury duty.

Except there's this blood pooling right here, that used to belong to someone.

You saw it, of course. But you're more safely distant than Carla.

I'll come back to you in a minute.

I mean to say it pokes Petey in the throat, deep despondency, to protect the Monster in this insurance investigation—all in the name of expediting the matter. He's had to be his brother's keeper too many times in his own interest. Yet he doesn't realize he's holding his own tail until it's too late. He doesn't follow how the Monster is only beginning to suffer.

The investigator spoke to the Monster, I think, just after the fire. I haven't verified this and don't wish to. He asked me if I knew the Monster's current whereabouts. He has more questions, presumably.

"My son and I are estranged," I replied, startling myself, and not just with my formality. "We have been so for a long time. I don't know where he is. Given my fragile health, I can't meet with him."

That woman might be able to run off to Michigan with Ollie. If Piper Lake becomes the next big mistake, she can always buy a plane ticket and return, can't she? There's always April and Howard's farm—and that cottage she could pay to have put up. And April's apiaries. Eternal honey . . . well, almost eternal, until it meets with something as commonplace as water.

WERE YOU THE kind of child who could punch a cat and then bring out a drawing you'd done of a dog—to smooth things over with the adult who might have disapproved of your behavior?

I've treated you so often like that, when it was treating time.

(I told you I'd get back to you. Don't underestimate the consoling satisfactions of a just-cleaned house. Or its ruthlessness, right?)

It took me some years—yes—but I finally asked myself what your family felt about your actions . . . and was it a loss for them, down there in that Kansas City you just shrugged off when I wanted one little story about it. (The only time you didn't have a tongue for the subject under discussion.)

And who finally found you?

And how many phenobarbitals had you actually taken?

I'd like to be precise about difficulty. You probably didn't know that about me. I learned it myself just recently, in the new life I'm falling into constantly, it seems.

I didn't open your note because I feared what it was going to ask of me. I feared anything it was going to claim.

Yes, I'm sure it would kill me.

You told me once, "I'm performing an experiment in human motivation and behavior." I thought you meant that as an artistic manifesto.

"Beaut the Smuggler"—what an address for a suicide note!

It's hard to pity you when you bring such pain, even this worn-down kind.

You and your delusions of grandeur—thinking you were nothing. And then thinking "they" were following you: the *Chicago Tribune*, the commies, the Klan, even J. Edgar Hoover.

All the time you thought I was impressed with your intelligence when, in fact, I was simply loving you. That was before you scared me away.

I let it out of me in a canoe at Lake Panorama, nineteen years after the fact.

I said I love you. I said I hate you.

I was with one of Miriam's grandkids, Sally, near the cove below the bluff, in the late afternoon. Sally might have heard me, though it was no more than whispering, and she was five at the time, so I doubt she could remember.

My whisper was like another blue knife, though I wouldn't have made that connection then.

I was just trying to get free of an old memory that had sprung upon me in the sunlight. That's all you could be then. I was just trying to let myself go from something that would like to be a secret—so it could be betrayed and finally understood.

By lying for everyone I can lie for myself, even for you.

I was trying to stop.

I probably smiled ironically to myself. Your child would have been nineteen, not this fair-haired little one in the bow.

I was being selfish in blessing poor me with such a vision.

It helped.

I could hear Ray and Al across the cove, shouting at the kids about keeping their life vests on.

Maybe I wasn't the only woman in your life, even at the end? There were all those other bare, languorous curves in your photographs—but the backgrounds were nearly all your apartment, anyone could see that. I remember the dank, peppery odor of those sheets after we'd slept in them. And the rank of the developing chemicals in your closet.

We think we're the one and only, don't we?

And maybe we'll make it so, at any price.

L ET ME TRY again.

When Carla was about twenty-one, just out of college but moving well on into her life away from home, we got into an argument about my covering for the Monster's antics. It had been brewing a good while.

"The lies, the lies never stop!" she snarled.

"Dear, it's not what you think," I said. "There's more to it. Really."

We went back and forth, past each other, she becoming only more and more enraged.

Finally she shouted, "I am so glad to be gone from this place . . . You know, I've hated you for years!"

Later, when she calmed down, she wept and begged me to understand, "I want you to live forever."

I was flummoxed by my worth. But something always reminds us, if we're unlucky (and also lucky).

I see now she wouldn't know what to do without forgiving me. Maybe she was also trying out some kind of goodbye, trying to leave behind the girl I'd encouraged her to be for so long.

She couldn't ask then: How important are lies to your love?

She's never acknowledged to me or anyone (at least anyone who's spoken to me) about that woman she's been sharing a house with out there in Santa Fe for how many years?

As if I would disapprove.

Maybe that's the new name she goes by.

A couple of years before the afternoon in the canoe, I thought I saw you. Ray had taken me to one of his distributor conventions in New Orleans—a reward to ourselves in the hope of doing better. We were sifting through crowds on Bourbon Street, among the neon and kid drunkenness. We were laughing and gawking, really holding the hands of a good time, as we did when we managed to find ourselves grateful together again or when one of Ray's extravagances had piled us into a car headlong to Mt. Rushmore or the Smoky Mountains on a summer morning.

Anyway, I thought I saw you, stepping out of a novelties shop. You, he, were with a black woman, a girl, really. I was amazed, and afraid. How could I have been wrong? How could you have faked your cold, cold cheek? You would have been in your mid-forties by then, and this man was maybe twenty-seven or twenty-eight.

Ray followed me as I chased you secretly in and out of three shops. I enthused about each gewgaw. And Ray probably thought I'd discovered in my excitement the silly-passionate girl he'd fallen for because he indulged my sudden interest in voodoo dolls and feathered hats. I could see he was enjoying the incongruity, pulled along, feeling generous and lucky I wanted something it was so easy for him to give just then. Ray among little plastic skeletons!

You could have met him!

(Oh, Ray, I remember how we'd seen those riots on TV so many years before, and the blacks marching for equality scattered when the fire hoses were turned on them, and how you'd say, "I can understand the coloreds want more, some of them deserve better than they have, but they don't need to be so angry about it." And how you'd tell those racist jokes from the office, to spite me. You never thought it was serious.)

But Ray would have understood, I think (after a few drinks, of course) what you meant when you'd stare at your open palms and make me do the same and say, "Look, isn't it amazing? What it's taken to make these . . . and how long to get to here . . . and this is you! You!"

At least he would have kept a respectful manner. And it would have sunk into him. Things like that did.

It didn't occur to me while I was shadowing you, or, really, your belated twin, that if you'd faked it, it meant you were letting me go.

If you'd faked it, it meant I wasn't guilty. It meant I'd wasted certain sidelong, backroom energies for years, and my own history was wrong.

A suicide is a gift that makes you selfish, possessive of it, the accusation in it.

But he wasn't you. That's probably why I wanted to watch him forever. To bring that shivery near.

We never got quite close enough to hear your banter. Ray was urgent to buy me that green boa I'd snatched up (to seal the moment of my joy with a souvenir), and so we stood in line at the cashier as you laughed your way out the door.

We have no idea what we mean to strangers we pass.

Carla wore that green boa to the Spinster's Spree her junior year at East.

What could I truly be guilty of, anyway? Running back to life?

I'm heading next door now, to find out what Shelby and Alana are watching on TV. Got to. I'll take a tray of Rice Krispies cookies as my battering ram.

MY OLD FRIEND Eleanor Hokin called today. I haven't heard from her in almost two years. My fault. I didn't want to explain how the Monster situation had gone from worse to weird. (All my small talk had expired and left me with closet weeping and a worthless confession about to pop at the wrong moment . . . so I didn't have the gumminess to fake happy for her. She hears it too well and doesn't hold back.)

Eleanor has macular degeneration now, though she can still see, she says, and she plays solitaire every morning with her first cup of coffee, to check if her eyes have gotten worse. One of her granddaughters is Army and stationed in Iraq. Eleanor is thankful the war has been declared over and is certain her progeny's progeny will be brought home soon. That's one I can hear too well, but I stopped my ears to it. She phoned me up, after all.

Eleanor's one of the Bolders from Ray's little group I came into when we married. I called them that, the ones who didn't act as I imagined most people nine or more years my senior were supposed to act. She'd mention something like her husband's testicles squirming against her thigh while he slept. Or she'd dab bourbon on her baby's gums to knock him out. I was impressed by her then and was still impressed twenty years ago when she assured me, "The great thing about being old is that so much doesn't matter anymore. Everyone is so concerned about how they look they aren't looking at you. Besides if you look bad, that makes them feel good, and they like that."

I keep that in mind when I secretly tear into a woman whose arms have flabbed enough to resemble mud slides.

I got to it, right away. "Well, I'm seeing someone." That's how I said it, as though we were twenty-five and proud to be getting pregnant finally. I think she could hear me grinning.

"Does he have a friend?" she asked. "Except for a few schnooks singing 'I Blow a Lot of Bubbles' at exercise time down at Dunes Care, there aren't any available men my age around here."

Eleanor's toes crinkle when she thinks she's gotten a good one in. They seem to clutch the ground. It was sweet to feel it just then. She married well, one of the boys with real family farm money who went to Iowa State after the war. Big Ag, she called him, or Ben the Smaller when they weren't getting along. He's one of the bubble-blowing singers now, these last four years. Alzheimer's. I don't know how she does it. I guess he's one of the calm ones. I've always imagined her lounging among some fat, red blossoms in the Florida sunlight. Her reward, as much as I could conjure. She always liked her flowers outsized, and she stuck with Big Ag through all his uncharming pursuits. She said she suspects there's a lot more dirt around her house she misses now, though she's had a cleaning lady for years. The kids also worry about her stepping onto unretrieved broken glass. She says she won't give them the relief of knowing she still can make out those cards at solitaire pretty well. She stayed with Ag for the money, that's for sure, but she never bought anything. At least, nothing for show.

I think she called to invite me down, though it's already sweltering there. She and Ag retired to Sanibel not long after Ray died, and I've always promised her I'd visit. Or maybe she hoped I'd invite her up here. She still has a daughter in Ames.

Maybe she didn't really get my number from Greta.

Maybe Petey gave it to her. Trying to coax me out of here in another direction? Maybe Kate's told him about Ollie and the UP.

"Go for it," Eleanor said, about Ollie. As though it were that simple, which it is, isn't it?

———

Just back from walking on Blue Jay Trail. I'm learning to ramble along on my own, though there were three young mothers pushing strollers who I kept in sight.

Greta, my perfect only sister who moved out to Scottsbluff twenty years ago, was with me, too, in mind. So I'll say it here, since you'll never meet her and maybe I never will again, either: I've never gotten entirely around the fact that she and Louis didn't at least make the first gesture toward taking Petey and April. She's six years older, and they were more established. And they couldn't have their own, anyway.

So there. I've said it. And now I'm petty.

It doesn't look as bad as I thought it would.

Our mother said not a word to her about Petey and April in my presence. I'm sure they pow-wowed on the topic, and Greta obeyed the drift. She was the talented one.

I supposed it trapped her.

Maybe she's a Carla . . . or Carla's a Greta.

She used to dress me up like her baby when we were little. She practiced the piano four or five hours a day, for Mother, until she hurt her hand.

Funny to realize now she must have been gone for good a long time before Phil got restless for California. All in the guise of going off to a better school.

Through my late teens, Phil and I were like the kids in the family. I hadn't lost her then, because I thought she was mine.

Funny to consider so late how unimportant you were.

Bah!

So MAYBE GRETA didn't really injure her hand. Maybe that was the story she invented to cut her chains to the piano. She never really came home afterward. And I couldn't tell you for sure which hand it was.

Wouldn't that be a knocker . . .

When did I come to believe she was chained to the piano and was so lucky to have gotten hurt? I believed she couldn't fathom how lucky she was. I thought she was taking her grief out on us all from far away—no hope for a musical career, etc. If she really had such a dream. She was so much older, it seemed. So much taller. She got most of our mother's poise, along with those eyes and good legs. When I came back from Chicago, from you, she wrote to me from Omaha. She invited me out there. She even called me. I could have told her what was happening.

Maybe she's always been happier than I've let her be.

OLLIE (driving through the countryside, near Winterset):
Friends should be like muses.

JILL (daydreaming, a little morose): What?

OLLIE: Like muses. They should inspire.

JILL: What? Inspire us to gossip?

OLLIE: No. I mean, inspire us to be more . . . encouraged, at
least.

JILL: What's wrong with just keeping company?

OLLIE: Not a thing.

(THE easy silence that is Ollie's forte ensues.)

JILL (predictably restless): Well, what about it?

OLLIE: What?

JILL: Inspiration, dummy!

OLLIE (grinning into the speedometer): I guess I've been
starving for some good surprise in life, until now. I don't
know . . .

JILL: That's my line.

OLLIE: What?

JILL: I don't know.

OLLIE: Don't you?

JILL (seizing the banterly chance, for a change): I think you do.

OLLIE: As often as I can.

JILL: Agreed.

(Mutual triumphant silence.)

Reasons for going to Piper Lake with Ollie:

1. The Monster. I've had it. What am I going to do with him anyway?
2. The house is gone. What's here for me? (Why not?)
3. Ollie's kind. He's tender. He likes to talk. He likes to listen. Even though he was a seminarian twenty-five years ago, he never brings up the usual God stuff. Never.
4. He's a pretty good lover. (Yes!!!)
5. He's a muse!

Reasons for not going to Piper Lake:

1. The Monster. All the usual reasons. (So what are they, Jill?)
2. The kids. Petey. April and Howard and the cottage. Kate. She needs some sane older woman in her life, even more now. Right.
3. Health. What about a doctor there?
4. Who is Laura Aussoway? (We've all seen *Unsolved Mysteries* on TV. And the crime shows where the old lady is seduced. Do I *really* know this man?)
5. Ollie's porn magazines hidden under his bed. What is it with that boy? Ray had a few in the garage, too.

What a pathetic list.

I was never good at making them. Not like Ray.

KATE WENT WITH ME for a scheduled peacemaker check at the clinic. Today, the man with the yellowed, fellow-smoker fingers taped the electrodes to my ankle and held the little disk against my chest and punched the buttons on the computer console.

"So, did you have a rough time last night?" he asked me.

He wasn't leering. Too bad.

"No," I replied.

Last night was just another lie down.

I didn't mention the weeping beforehand. One of the gooey sumping-ups that press hard and hot when I remember by accident . . . in this instance: recalling how I recognized Ray was in the next aisle over from me at Target once, by the way he cleared his throat.

There wasn't anything rarified about it.

Yellow Fingers told me that last night and lately, according to the record, the peacemaker kicks in 16% of the time, and mostly at night, nudging me along through dreamland.

I'd be dead without it, he didn't say but implied.

So many numbers on the readout, I don't guess what they mean. I want to believe no one can explain them. Add them up and write a check for that amount and then tear it up. That will do.

We all could use a thousand years to consider even the clearing of a throat. I mentioned that to Kate, and she squinted at me curiously through the air between us for a second, because I was out of character.

THE MONSTER'S BEEN calling, and I still haven't been answering. Sometimes he begs. Sometimes he shouts. I've erased a couple of his messages after the first snarl. It's peculiar that I feel I'm hurting us all when I do it.

I've almost confided this to Ollie.

This morning I stepped out to catch Shelby as she was going off to work and give her a top for Alana I picked up yesterday at T.J. Maxx, and I swear I spotted Cane Toad's pickup skulking at the end of the cul-de-sac.

For the record (I know too well what I'm afraid of) this is Friday, May 9th.

WHY DO WE THINK it's so bad to close our eyes forever? Why do we have to fight everyone about it while our eyes are open?

Rain now. The trees in the wind, wadding and unwadding themselves.

PRIL AND HOWARD had us all (Petey and Jane and the kids, too) out to the farm for Mother's Day. It was so balmy we picnicked under the cottonwoods—Howard's idea (a last-minute inspiration, April said). Howard's sly in his dimples, and it's easy to mistake his clumsiness for crudeness because he pretends he's made of chainsaw oil and Iowa State football highlights. You would have despised him, and you'd have been wrong to.

I got the notion going in the family some years ago that Howard resembles my officially announced first love, Terry Jenkins, in the eyes, and maybe he does, by now. It's been so long.

Things like that sweeten the scene with Howard, and I think it makes April happier somewhere, even if it means she'll force more presents on me, to coax from me what she can't figure out she wants. I had the same quandary with my mother. You simply don't wish to be so alone in your confusion. But Mother can't, or won't, help you, pity it is to admit. The whole matter becomes like some old, spoiled lipstick, with that waxy, rotted odor. You should throw it out. But you keep it because you believe more eyes than you could wish for suddenly lapped at you in that color, and now it's been discontinued, and you want to remember it because you always hope to find it again, out of habit checking every clearance bin that happens along.

Anyway, Howard had a rough boyhood. It's taken very little to make him happy with me. I rarely miss the opportunities. With Howard, I'm like the fellow in Florida that Eleanor was roaring over the other day. He wears a life vest pinned with dollar bills and stands on the street corner and gives out from a wad he carries with him. He's loaded, so he likes to see people smile.

This was the first Mother's Day in years we've been together. I suppose it's because they all wondered whether it might not be the last, given my cardio behavior of late. Petey and Jane presented me with the most simpering greeting card. Jane picks them out. The sweeter they are the more she hates me. The flowers on this one, purple and swirling, and the gold lettering (a funereal kiss-off) said: *To a glorious mother, for all the things you do . . .*

Or some such tripe.

I made sure to forget to take it with me when I left there tonight.

But the kids played Frisbee in the poplars, and Howard cranked up homemade ice cream. And later we actually knocked around a few croquet balls. (It made me want to at least rent some new golf clubs and dare a swing.)

Petey took my arm for a walk to inform me that the insurance investigator is still holding back on closing the case, and the law might yet be summoned. There is more to this story, of course, but I can do without it.

He asked if I'd heard from the Monster.

I paused then told him yes but that I hadn't talked to him and that I meant not to. I had other plans now.

That stopped him more abruptly than I'd hoped.

"I think I'll be taking a trip," I said, "just going for awhile. Ollie and I. In a few weeks."

"Do you think that's really wise . . . I mean, considering your health?"

"I think it's overdue, dear," I said. "How long have you and Carla been after me to make some changes?"

I looked at him, more anxious than anyone should be about her own consent, and I dug down into my mother bag, as though he'd come to me with a question about asking girls out.

"You know," I said. "Everything changes, dear, sooner or later."

What could he say? Even though I had no idea beforehand that I was ready to announce about Ollie and Piper Lake. There was no choice but to take Petey's arm again and squeeze it and walk us on. I'm not exactly in collapse, if he only knew.

Carla phoned in about dessert time. April and Howard must have arranged it, given the congruence. Carla loves Ray ever-most when she thinks she hears me claiming some old affection of his. She believes I left him for my Drears, and I did, for awhile. You'd think she became the wife then. Well . . . she was, to an adolescent loneliness in them both. (The kind she won't countenance in me or anyone else. How's that for poetic jaw-snap?)

I don't think she could tell you, for instance, that the sycamore was Ray's favorite tree, or even that he had a favorite tree. Or that he grieved on the dock at the lake for a hurt he gave her that had caused her to storm off in her car for three days when she was about nineteen. What it was he wouldn't tell me. I imagine he thought I'd hurt us all with it, impulsively. Probably I would have.

Ray could be a pleaser. Though he hated grapefruit, he'd ac-cept a fat bag of them from a friend because he imagined great affronts in certain kinds of honesty. I'm sure, at least, Carla doesn't know how the goose pimples on my thigh vanished under his hand in the night. She'd better not.

I've "misguided" myself here. A little razzmatazzing like that has come to entertain me too much, icing any bruise behind it (if that's where the bruise hides, if it is. Oh, it is.). But I don't have an alternative. I should probably just stop it, in the middle. Like this

———

But it isn't the middle, is it? Even though it always feels that way. And this apartment's now in the hour of childhood melancholy, the very purple snow. It's lonely here after the presence of so many people there, and who hasn't felt that before?

Ray would say, on occasion, that if he hadn't married me, he'd be dead. He said he meant he would have worked all the time, or stayed up night after night, or not eaten well. He wouldn't have had any structure in his life. And so he learned to cook by knowing me, because I did it so well, he said. (One of his dauntless lies.) He organized his time more stringently in those periods when I did not. (To-do lists that got done!) My ineptitudes, if I can call them that, changed his life. Carla didn't appreciate those benefits. Did anyone?

I should stop this. After all, Carla sent me a gift basket with my favorite Polish vodka. (I'd sample some now, but I'm afraid of drowning alone in the stuff, like Alberta Sarnac's parakeet.) And Carla and I both laughed today when quite by accident I reminded her of Barbara Jenner finding the envelope marked "Carla's tooth" in her rose bushes. I never figured out where Carla got the idea her tooth was supposed to go under a bush and not under her pillow. She hadn't heard the part about Barbara until today, but she enjoyed elaborating on how she sneaked over there the next morning to discover the envelope with the quarter I'd put in from the tooth fairy.

"That was magical," she sighed, really sighed, "more than any of the Santa Claus business . . . I carried that coin around all day. I wouldn't put it in my pocket. God, I didn't want to lose it! . . . And I wanted to spend it so badly. But not just on candy."

Some lucky timing there, even now. Thank you, Barbara.

I'm exhausted, but I need to tell what I first intended to mention here. At my request, Ollie came over to April's at about five, for an hour or so. (He couldn't stay longer because he has a deadline on some computer job tonight, and I wanted him to have a quick out anyway. This was supposed to be a plunge, not a loll.) Of course, Petey has met him before, two or three times. But the sight of him in April's living room, beside the giant-screen TV blaring the Cubs game! It all seemed like—what?—Day One in a new school . . . or maybe the way a son feels when he has to endure for the first time seeing his mother dancing in public. I was embarrassed . . . and proud . . . and all of it seemed mirror-sideways. Just to hear him chat with Jane about the new blue bridges over the freeway expansion downtown . . . or watch him go off on his own to the stables with Howard . . . I could feel myself hoping Kate would like him very much.

April sent three jars of her honey with him. I kissed him good-bye, there in the driveway, with everyone waiting to wave him off. Why not pull up this particular shade and throw open the windows?

I called him after I got home, for just a minute.

"They're lovely people," he said solemnly.

PPARENTLY, THE MONSTER showed up at April's the other evening, just after I left. He was drunk and perhaps otherwise altered, and he claimed he'd brought a present for me.

Kate (who had time for me and Blue Jay Trail this morning because classes at the community college let out on Friday
and her Stephen is away on some "retreat") said April marched
into the house right away, and Petey went out to the road to talk
to the Monster.

They ended up in a shouting match, Kate said, and Howard
had to pull Petey back, to keep them from having an actual fight.
Petey can flare and believe he's still the bigger brother.

Kate said, "Dad didn't believe Uncle Peter when he told him
you weren't there. And then Dad wanted to know where you
were living. Uncle Peter said he would deliver the gift, but Dad
wouldn't give it to him."

Evidently, the Monster had a little wrapped-up box. Howard
managed to convince him that he would pass it to me, though
Petey ended up with it.

Kate said, "Uncle Peter said something to Dad like 'You've
become such a stranger to us all,' and when he tore off in the
truck, Dad shouted back, 'You're a stranger, too!'"

Of course, I wonder about Kate seeing her father like that—

how many times? She said she didn't think her father noticed she was present, though she also said it was getting dark, and she'd stayed back beside one of the pines along the driveway. Yes, she can reel off something blasé, like "Dad doesn't get that he's just a target market for drug dealers. He still thinks he's some star or something." But anyone could see today how she ached to ask me what he really thinks he is (as if I knew), and how he got to be as he is, how it started, and before. She just hasn't learned yet where to place those questions so they can't be evaded.

I didn't help her out, I confess.

I suppose I could have mentioned that her father told me once that Petey got him high the first time, when he was about fifteen.

"Not that I'm blaming him for my mistakes or my habits," he was quick to add. (This was after his first rehab, when he was just learning to operate such lingo.)

Better, I could have mentioned (probably should have mentioned) that boy in the airport the other day when I took Miriam for her flight to Costa Rica. He was about seven, and he wore a superhero mask too broad for his face that swooped out like cat-eye glasses above his cheeks and a black cape now and then skirting the floor, and he was flying around and around and punching the air, half tumbling in his clumsiness, whipping the villains in the dream of who he was being. He didn't notice anyone or anything actually around him, except maybe a wall or chair he was about to collide with (and there were moments when I wasn't sure he would manage even that).

His father, slouching-bored with the bags, let him play on and on . . . probably so he would sleep on the flight.

The boy was cute, of course. Just so, so much. And that (given the usual void of the airport scene) was enough to get anyone watching. But I kept on, even as Miriam fussed through her carry-on for a pill, because I could hardly stand how this sudden misery throbbed through me, something like downdrafts that shoot glitter across smooth, dark lake water. It's even odder now that I realize I more or less forgot it by the time I'd hugged Miriam goodbye and was wandering the parking garage for my car. As I watched that boy I probably thought of the Monster and Petey dressed up for Halloween, or how they resembled little men in their Easter suits the year we took them and the girls on the Rock Island Rocket to Omaha. I had to be thinking of them, somewhere. But now I remember only thinking the boy understood everything he needed to understand as long as those who made up the rest of things were there around him understanding (or misunderstanding) as we do. He was moving around in the story he was given, wasn't he? And he loved it more than anything else right then, so much so he was inside his love for it, the way we're inside those loves we don't realize exist while we're inside them.

But I didn't mention this incident to Kate because the Monster hasn't given her a birthday present in a few years.

If she were of a certain mind, like Carla, for instance, she could blame me for that.

It would be a shallow blame, but that's the kind people drown in most often.

ORNING SEVENTY-THREE HERE, among my imperson-
al walls (though who's counting?).

And I'm wondering what's in the little gift box the Monster brought to April's and (because I'm habitual) whose
truck the Monster was driving the other evening. His last vehicle
was repossessed months ago, and he has half the bank credit of
a snail.

I'm foolish this way today because (let's just try it out) my
mother was one of the lovely, strong women. She had com-
posure, a slight, almost aristocratic pause before she spoke. It
seemed she could order death around.

And because the Monster wouldn't let me protect him. I only
thought I was helping myself to him, especially after Ray was
gone.

Near the end, my mother's voice was like a piece of shaken
aluminum foil. I hear it in my own voice now and then, the same
way I turned my face from her eyes and wet hair in the big mirror across from the tub when I stepped out of the shower this
morning. There was no mirror of that sort in my lost house, so I
never saw what was to be seen only by me from somewhere just

in front of me. I guess that's one more gift of the fire, in exchange for the takeaways.

Even Mother didn't deserve that voice.

Or the way I'm treating her just now.

Luckily she won't mind.

But it would have been easy to tell if she had minded. I've never been as graceful, or accurate, in delivering disapproval. She was helpless to be otherwise.

I could never have told her that.

Nor could Greta, before and after she finally ran off to live as one of the Jesus-breeders Mother preached against. She remained with them even after she returned home for the duration.

It's been a long time coming to this particular halt.

So where am I in my dignity? Some people even sneeze like their parents.

You see what I've been talking about, right?

Inform me, please. (I'm not asking Mother.)

———

The Monster was twenty-seven when Ray died, and at the very least a few awful things happened to him while incarcerated, some of them sexual. He's alluded to them on occasion, to get the upper hand in certain crises. I always felt the twinge when I remembered how grateful I was to the court for hauling him off. When Ray was ill, especially. The Monster couldn't believe his father was going to die . . . Even underneath his most piled-up highs he realized this lack, I'm sure. And Ray seemed to hurry on to death, though he fought hard at the end in spite of himself, and I thought he'd wanted to escape the maze I'd let the Monster lead us into. In a few tearing-up instances, I considered his passing a revenge, or even a final summation of regret like: this is not what we could have ended up with, the two of us on this summer day.

———

Of course, right away I'd planned to tell the Monster face-to-face that his father was dead. I didn't want him hearing it from Sheila or anyone else. Petey went with me to visiting hours. But the Monster had already learned about it from the watchdogs there. They'd used it on him, I think, though the Monster hadn't spoken to Ray in several years. And he was not himself.

———

So that was that. What else could it be?

———

The afternoon Ray was diagnosed, October 14, 1991, we drove home without talking. They'd given him six months. Several times he turned the car radio up and then down, as though he were bringing the music (or whatever it had made him think of) closer for a moment. He was a man who'd always tried to have his shirt tucked in. He'd been a calm boy, his mother said, with terrible acne. There were clusters of scars in the middle of his cheeks, just a few, like the holes in the top of a pie crust. Those had always been reminders to me that he'd been a boy. That and when he tried to sing. I always felt sorry for him then.

I wanted to touch him there, but instead I took his hand. That's one of the images I realize I've kept of him. I suppose I should notice that tendency, now that most of my snapshots of him are gone. Not that I went through the albums very often. I'm not one for pressing flowers, maybe only a couple of weeds.

We came home, and he mentioned how messy the garage was and how he ought to rake the backyard, but he already had some strong pain below. The Monster was out somewhere, for days, I think, and we did something rare for us. We lay down together and slept there in the late afternoon light, fully dressed. The leaves overhead had already changed, but the rains hadn't knocked them off yet.

I think of that stillness, how you doze and wake and don't want to move even a single muscle because as soon as you do your life resumes. Of course we were scared, though I can't quite feel it anymore. I merely know it happened because I was there and I've told myself so ever since.

A few days later, I came home and found him sitting at the hall closet, combing out old Christmas tinsel with his fingers. He'd decided we would have a final family holiday. We did our best. I think the kids would agree. As he worked on the tinsel, he tried to explain to me how it didn't make him sad exactly but astonished.

———

And now I've decided I'm going to call Ollie and arrange a little shopping trip for new clothes for Piper Lake. I was inside most of this last winter, you know, and I still haven't shaken off the cruddy nightgown feeling.

I T'S 3:29 A.M.

And has been for years.

I'm just usually better asleep than now.

I mean that you can't let yourself very far into noticing. You can't really pay attention to the thumping bed next door at Shelby's, or to the fact that each leaf and worm and downshifting truck, every face in the grocery store has a history and a future with a big pendulum swinging around in it, a white-hot pendulum or one as frigid and old and pure and slow to melt as any chunk of Antarctica.

Or both.

The thing swings in you, too, grazing you until you can't bear it.

I stared at the TV screen but didn't turn it on. Good for me. I don't need any more war news. Or victory news. That's what they might be calling it right now.

Kate went shopping with me yesterday for Piper Lake attire. She'd wolf-whistled when I'd kissed Ollie goodbye in April's driveway, so I'm very approving of her at the moment. I should have expected this, since I would never have met him in that dumb little writing class at the community college if she hadn't been attending school there herself and urged me to sign up. I suppose that makes me cowardly. But after creeping around above the Monster and Cane Toad, maybe it was a sign of new life coming, even before I decided to flatline.

People always wonder, afterward, how they could have stared out at their heart's desire so long from over the shoulder of whatever it was they were having to hug.

Odd, too, how you can suddenly meet the person you were (or remember you were) before you became the person who seems to have just fallen away from you. In my case, this reacquaintance isn't really that young woman me. But some of her is rescued, maybe, or dug up. Can't that be so? There are my new bags in the corner. And two pairs of pedal pushers that feel kind on me. And two new sweaters. Of course, I need a fresh closet of resolutions. But I'm going, and I'm smiling. Even if Ollie really finds me out or reveals himself to be a bigamist serial killer and I'm back here in town in two weeks, I'm letting this place go, despite the lease. Sorry, Shelby. (I hope that's not Ricardo you've let back into your bed.)

I've considered showing some of these pages to Ollie. And that scares me, since they keep making me stranger and stranger in a way I quite enjoy.

Because they can get me into a misunderstanding I allow (for a change).

You used to say: "Oh, c'mon. Just one lick," even if the matter in question was whether or not to take a walk along Grant Park in the rain. And that would jar me from my little obsessions and my focus on gathering the floating feathers of what might happen tomorrow. You were most right for me that way.

When I didn't want to see those first pictures you'd taken of me ghost up in the darkroom basin (and they were, I admit, gorgeous, shadowy images), you said, "I'm partly trying to capture your reluctance. And your bewilderment."

A girl doesn't forget that.

You said, "It's just a little light on paper."

Of course, once we got going, I was eager to display my wares (instead of my wears and tears now), but you slowed me down. I was flattered. I guess I wanted to be frightened, too. I needed to learn if I could trust you with the bits of me I thought I was offering across those weird distances. Or maybe I wanted to give up holding so tight to my untrustworthy self. I guess I hoped to learn what those bits were made of. I insist I can still feel the candle-heat ripple across my shoulder blades. On only a half-glass of wine.

Did I end up in any stag magazines? "Art" had to pay your rent sometime, right?

How about THOSE documents for the Smithsonian archives!

I knew I might really love you when you let me try to take pictures of you. You didn't like being on the other side, no matter how blasé you tried to act. So silly, you trying to cover up your body made anonymous. And I was sorry for you, a little. But it was a lick, too. Those pictures of your thigh so up close they came out blurry. I let you burn those negatives because I thought I'd get another chance to try out that part of us.

Did we even know we were alive?

Beaut and Beaut, playing this way.

No one else could call us that again.

Time: 4:13 a.m.

Place:

Further (perhaps better) reasons for going to Piper Lake with Ollie:

1. When he enters an elevator, he tries to not turn his back to the people already on it. (Not that we're likely to encounter elevators at Piper Lake.)

2. He loves the blue driftwood color of winter fields. By mentioning this, I found out I do, too. (So what else is there to find out I love?)

3. When he's alert to the situation (which he often is, provided he's away from the computer screen), he touches me more often before I touch him. That's the way it is. (And he lets me exfoliate his shoulders in the shower.)

4. Once, when the truly stupid terror came on me (that maybe that was a real chest pain just now and my heart is going to stop), I didn't let on but tossed out something like: "It's funny how things don't want to stay still . . . Here's spring again . . ." He caught on and offered a sip of his Pepsi

and said, "Rhythm is God's kindness to us . . . if there is a God, of course."

5. He doesn't have any photos of Piper Lake. And who wants to imagine and be disappointed in person? It's my second lake in life, after all. So I go to it soon or forget it.

6. We were driving near the capitol building, and he asked to see the house I grew up in across from Union Park. I hadn't passed by it in years. The place looks like a bad smell now, warped and dingy, a Victorian heap, with plastic siding cracked like rotted Tupperware (and the inside cut up long ago into apartments for poor gomers-in-the-making, I think). But it's outlasted my marriage house. And the neighborhood is still beautiful in many places, thanks to rehab missionaries and other such romantics. The park still rolls away from those porches serenely. We tooled around the handful of circles and then stopped and strolled. I showed him where Phil and Greta and I made snowmen. (They tried to roll me up in one.) I revealed to him the not-so-secret "secret" catwalk (still in business, amazingly!) and the knoll with the now-decimated pine trees we always ran past on our way home from school. Funny, how much you do now (any now) that you might be giving a tour through one day. Anyway, it wasn't long before I was trying to describe how the silhouette of the busted chandelier in the bedroom Greta and I shared sometimes looked like a fountain and sometimes like flowers. I tried to explain about the little balcony I could get to by scuttling through the attic closet. It had a balustrade as though it were a real balcony and not just a perch overlooking a narrow stairway lit by a small frosted window

where I would read for hours. The point here is that Ollie was interested enough in this dust because it's mine, ordinary dust in every other way. Petey can't understand this since he's convinced that I've drafted Ollie to substitute for the Monster. And after so long with Jane, there's a part of him that's become accustomed to believing in people as tools we secretly pray to as we use them. Anyway, that twenty minutes in Union Park is probably as close to Laurel Hill as Ollie and I need to get.

W**E WERE WAITING** at Jiffy Lube, and I turned to him, "So, who is Laura Aussoway?"

I'm getting impulsive. It's my heart, I told him, but he's not buying that line. Not for my snoopiness, in this case. I pleaded that I hadn't read any of the letters, which is true. I only noticed the return address on the envelopes. (After all, they were rubber-banded and stacked like bills at the mint, who could miss them?) It was the first time I've seen him almost helplessly angry, those ball bearings crowding at the hinge of his jaws as he kept his mouth shut and probably summoned some ritual from his seminary days that's helped him around his dragon.

I'd hurt him, and I was sorry and said so. We've tried to keep hands off each other's unmentioned items, but this wisdom flops, sooner or later.

Anyway, he stayed clenched for some time. It was a little re-minder of what Ray had to sop up from my Drears. I kept think-ing of that over and over. The man has charm, so why should I squander it with my flaws?

Petey, it turns out, had visited Ollie's place the night before, with only five minutes warning. He said he respected Ollie but wanted him to understand that I'd been seriously ill, that I had financial problems, that he and April and Carla were very worried about my welfare.

Ollie must have had to summon up his dragon-spooking ritual at that point, too, because he worked to relate this news without laying into Petey, and he ached to. Ollie assumes people will first be nice, almost out of habit. So he gets mournfully surprised and yet can't quite remember it afterward, since the hope or reflex is so deep in him.

Of course, Petey meant three-quarters well. He also wanted to inspect Ollie's domicile, prying for arguments against him he could bring to me like a cat with a rat. He's probably driven past Ollie's place dozens of times since he jarred the address out of me.

I can hear his business tone, the one we think covers jealousy best.

I can't say I'm outraged by his rudeness. I'm glad he still needs me this much in his Jane-run world. It's good Ollie hears I'm wanted elsewhere, and by someone not stuck through with guilty mother love.

As nearly as I can fathom from Ollie, Petey hadn't figured out beforehand a clear objective for his visit (aside from maybe revealing Ollie to be a cad who would dump me without even a sticky note: "So long, sister!"). This fuzziness is almost out of character enough to bring me around to the tenderness that boy's always deserved. (But I can't help you this time, Petey. I'm not siding with Ollie. I'm just going to Piper Lake to see. You can't understand how much I need it. I can't understand. And I'm not bringing up your intrusion for discussion.)

Maybe Ollie put those letters from Laura Aussoway out for me to see. (Yes, yes, people adore a convenient explanation like that.)

Ollie said he assured Petey he respected everyone's concern . . . and he hoped everyone realized how much he cared for me . . . and that the sweet air at Piper Lake would fortify me.

How much he cared for me.

I assume he actually used that phrase with Petey. It's a disappointment, but I wouldn't have said "love," either. And he has more reason to shy from using that word than I do.

It's not necessary now.

Or maybe anymore.

I do believe he actually used the word "fortify," too.

He said Petey seemed unprepared for conciliation of any sort. He guesses Petey thought he would dismiss him with, "Your mother's old enough to make up her own mind."

Which is obvious, to Ollie and me at least.

(Truth be told, on every visit to this apartment, Petey sneaks glances for signs of my commencing infirmity, physical or mental, it doesn't seem to matter which. The problem will be made apparent, I infer, from a grimy coffee pot or spider webs in six or more corners. No, folks, you don't need to put the pet parrot in the freezer anymore.)

Who knows what else Petey and Ollie really said. As Ollie went on about it, still upset, I thought of how boys, when they hit puberty, suddenly become shy about the shower room. And about Petey and the Monster (one clipped and the other not). They were never young enough together to share the bathtub. (Glad I didn't have to answer those questions.)

The point isn't that Petey left Ollie's dissatisfied or peeved, though I wonder if Ollie thought I might have engineered the meeting as some girlish test. I don't think he would actually believe that, but he could entertain the possibility, given my ill-timed elbowing about Laura Aussoway. He was very courtly with me around his silences. I have a lot to learn about that man, if life will let me.

The point is that Ollie told me as much as he finally did about Laura Aussoway.

Who can he have ever trusted with this history, if he's trusted anyone?

No one's trusted me like this, even Ray.

I thanked him. That sounds silly, I know, but what else do you dare when you're made to realize someone is suddenly there, existing against every likelihood, and you're even ashamed you ever sweetly called him a bozo, because you assumed you understood what being alive involved for anyone?

You'll never see a story like Ollie's in the newspaper.

Or here, either.

He didn't ask me to keep it private, but that vow is more than I deserve. It makes me think I must be a chance for him.

I wouldn't know where to start to tell anyway.

Petey would have me warehoused if he found out.

I'll only say it's amazing Ollie's even made the place he has for himself, and it's no shock he's pretty much alone. Every day, people let their own flesh fall away for less.

Where his touch has been.

I'll have to figure out how to stop thinking about that.

There he was, carrying my lipstick in his pocket.

What kind of story did he ever imagine he could write for that class at the community college?

Must sleep, now. Try.

FOR SOMEONE WHO couldn't get the idea of time, or enough time, I suddenly have it stacked up around me like boxes for the Disabled American Veterans.

I crossed Pleasant Hill Road at the entrance to Blue Jay Trail, and I thought: If I stumble, this approaching car will smash me.

Then I saw myself trying to trot, suddenly desperate, and tripping, tumbling and the rest of it. And I shivered and actually whipped my head like a cat breaking a mouse neck in its jaws. (I must have looked like a lunatic, twitching, muttering to the air.)

This occurred today, and I realize now it occurs every time I cross Pleasant Hill Road at the entrance to Blue Jay Trail.

Like the idea that perks up when I pass the bagel shop beside Hy-Vee. I remember April joking that Howard eats the identical breakfast every morning.

"He's just like a dog," she said.

Every time, that comes to me.

And then tucks itself behind the next moment. Gone. Seemingly, if you notice.

Things muck out from under your heels. Suddenly your hair coloring has leached away toward an awful revelation because you missed the salon appointment you've kept like a clock cuckoo for years, even with the Monster and Cane Toad cooking their craziness in the basement. You missed it, just like that, without a hint.

But you remember (briefly, over and over) Howard is a breakfast dog.

Kate repeats, "Dad says he loves me. When I see him, he always tells me that."

I don't believe he took the opportunity do so the other night at April's.

My son.

Ollie might not have divulged Laura Aussoway, ever.

He wasn't required to answer.

Am I about as much as he feels he deserves? After everything? Stuff that.

OLLIE (urging Jill to stop treating him like fragile, semi-
    reassembled pottery because of Laura Aussoway): In the
    end, it's just not *that* special. Everybody has their burden.
    Everybody has something they can never really overcome,
    or finish.
JILL: I wish I believed that.
OLLIE: Believe it.
(HE grins.)
JILL: I suppose it helps to.
(SHE checks to see if he follows.)
JILL: If everybody suffers the same, a person's suffering doesn't
    mean anything.
OLLIE: It doesn't stand out, sure. But that doesn't make it
    meaningless.

JILL (quick): It makes it like breathing!

OLLIE: Well?

JILL: (Silence)

OLLIE: Why don't you go back to giving me a hard time? And I'll go back to enjoying it.

W'RE DECIDED—TO PIPER LAKE in two weeks, just after Memorial Day. Ollie says it might still be chilly (he hasn't been there this early in nearly ten years), but only off and on. Shelby was sorry to hear I was leaving. I didn't mention I saw Stretch-pants Man stumble from her door at 5:30 the other morning. Maybe she's definitively ditched Ricardo, but not for carpet samples, I hope. Stretch-pants Man must have grinned through his shaving lather for the blessing she gave him. At least twenty-five years difference between them.

Everyone's learning, or not, all the time.

Shelby could do worse, and has.

Anyway, Petey doesn't savor the idea of taking back the few bits of furniture here. I suggested he cart them to the Salvation Army, but he insisted I might need them (which is true). That's how he keeps informing me of his doubt. It's also one of his hundred entrées to observations that too much unfinished business is lying around my life for me to adjourn with Ollie like this. I let him talk. I can still do that for him.

I can also not bring up his tangle with Ollie, though he must assume I've been enlightened. He caught me on my way out this afternoon, dropping off the gift he cajoled from the Monster on

Mother's Day. I hadn't asked him about it before. (That would have just juiced up Jane too much in my imagination.) I probably was also wondering if he would really deliver it. Fortunately, we tripped right away onto furniture stowage, and I didn't have to open it in front of him. It doesn't help him to receive another opportunity to pity the Monster and give me that *voila!* mouth curl when the Monster's gift turns out to be flaking bars of waxy rose soap from Big Lots.

Okay. Perhaps it was two smidgens mean of me. That's privacy, too.

There isn't much left to pack here, really. Ollie's retaining his room in the apartment house, and he offered to store my smaller gear there, but I declined. We're not ready for that, truly, just like I haven't wanted him setting up an email account for me on this computer. He understands too well the inner workings of these diabolical machines, and I certainly don't. Call me untrusting, but he'd be too close to this. And it's too easy for me to lose track of where things are. I do that so well, already.

I guess I have room in my bags for the Eleanor Roosevelt fridge magnet, for its advice, at least.

The Monster's gift isn't rose soap this time. The package is too small and light for that, which is the reason it's still unopened here beside the keyboard. No ribbon or bow, but it's clearly the Monster's personal work, the pink paper meticulously folded. All edges true, like his walls and ceilings when he still could get up early for construction.

Why should a mother be shy of opening a little box from her son?

Next time he calls, I answer.

Some might say I should fear Ollie, for his past.

Some might say I should despise my son for ignoring me fallen and dying.

Some might say that you—yes, you—are more dead than all my talking to you and all your discretion can make otherwise, and you need to understand that fact now, no matter how long it's been.

Dreadful playthings—thoughts.

Ray had a past, too. It was named Janice. He met her not long after he got out of the army. Some of the Bolders had known her. She and Ray came within a week of the altar. But she wanted back into the wonder cave of County Seat, Minnesota, and he let her go, he said, thinking she'd return when she found it oddly shrunken, with a good number of her old friends pregnant and gossiping at the laundromat. He probably drove through that town more than once on business.

How he kissed my shoulder in the night to get me to turn toward him.

"They go at their own pace," the hospice nurse whispered, as though Ray or anyone calibrated precisely their passing.

He ran away from me more than once by wrapping us in a thick kindness. That's how we understood he would never leave me, whatever our threats.

I saw him lust in sorrow. It hurt, just enough, like marching to the horizon with the calluses too deeply shaved off your heels. He should be first among my dead.

I love all my children as much as I can, and they love me and each other as much as they can. But our resources trouble us.

April either foraged through or happened upon some of my private things while I was in the hospital for my hysterectomy and she was packing for college. She found the copy of my two letters to Phil demanding that he take his children back and, if he could stand it, adopt them out. I wrote them during those first weeks the kids were staying with us, when they were supposedly still just on vacation, because I thought he should choose and be responsible, not leave it on our doorstep after dark. (Of course, he had chosen—to make me choose.) I kept copies because I thought we might need them for any legal matters. I was a careful fool. Ray never learned of them, as far as I can discern, but April must have shown them to Carla. That's my theory, at least, because Carla and I fell on angry teeth about that time. I remember her bringing a group of Liberian exchange students from one of her college clubs for a backyard cookout at our place. Ray officiated over the hot dogs. The locust blossoms snowed on our foreheads, and we all enjoyed. She was trying to broaden us, in her mind. You know, exposing us to black people, and from afar. It happens. A child (almost still an infant, really) stares at you with those big eyes that seem to come from the first judgment. What is she thinking? You might as well ask a sparrow.

After his divorce, the Monster once wailed at me, "You can't know what this feels like!"

That's a fine trombone laugh. But true, if the notion is allowed to linger.

To think I could send Carla or that boy, when they were nine or ten, to Outlook Park Grocery for cigarettes, with just a note, and Andy there would sell them, no problem, and they would bring them to me.

WELL, I OPENED IT.

Mother's wedding ring.

She'd pressed it into my palm a few days before she died. The Monster hocked it five years ago with everything else he'd cleaned out of my jewelry box. (When he finally confessed to the theft, it was too late to get the stuff back.)

So how did he find it now?

A gift certificate to Pier One. That's what I'll tell Petey it was.

Shouldn't I also reform my untoward habit of fact substitution in these personal jams, since I'm flush with new experiments?

Of course that boy burned my house. How many times.

He'd be happy for an iota of my fury right now, it seems. It would constitute an answer. He's still learning from Cane Toad, I bet.

My mother had been wearing that ring almost fifty years. She said it would be wasted in the box with her, just like the new clothes she'd never worn in life that would be dressing her body.

Maybe Kate would like it. Somehow it's not mine to have back.

All these boxes.

Thunder now, distant. Oh, that's a timely effect, Jill. Did you order it?

I think I'll step outside and try to smell some lightning for a change.

A POSTCARD FROM MIRIAM, in Monteverde, the cloud forest. She's seen a motmot. It has a long featherless tail, except for an aquamarine flare on the tip, and it nests, she says, in a hole in the ground. She's also seen a scorpion and something called an agouti.

Well, Miriam, an article in today's paper says that a hair goes gray because air penetrates it.

How about that?

I won't be around to ahh your snapshots when you get back. I'm glad I won't have to explain in person. Ollie's not a boy-guide.

You'll have to call your daughter to pick you up at the airport.

If we only really wished people were here, when we wrote that to them.

———

Petey's informed me that Frank Garcia, our lawyer, thinks the insurance company is about to deny my claim and will try to prove arson. When the adjustor walked me around the place with the video camera a few months back, that was just the start of their investigation. They've talked to Barbara Jenner and the

Ericksons and Dunskys about any strange goings-on prior. I've spoken to Barbara about that conversation. She was sunny in her overcast, as you might expect. I don't believe she told much of the awful. She has too much neighborhood house-pride herself, and she believes hard words on another become boomerangs. Like most of us, she prefers others to pour her poisons into the stream. Besides, she saw me creeping over the weirdness there long enough she's decided I've been duly punished for my early years of having a good figure on our little league Saturdays and, I'll admit it, showing off home decorating (when I still thought it would save me).

I've tried to meet the insurance company's requests, even down to itemizing what was lost. That's an old, bad joke, of course. Nobody gets it, so it keeps getting told.

Luckily, Petey hired his own investigator to comb over the house before it was bulldozed. He didn't tell me this until now.

"I lost your house once," he said, with such humiliation in his voice and, really, heroism. "I couldn't let that happen again."

Lucky, too, I didn't turn in a claim on the jewelry the Monster stole when he took my mother's ring. I've never asked the insurance for a penny, though the Monster pushed me to try, on occasion. I wasn't joining him in fraud. That kind, at least.

Petey's no quitter in matters like this. He made his move.

"It wouldn't look good if you left town right now," he said, "if we're facing some litigation."

The insurance company wants me to undergo an Examination Under Oath. Right away.

Before they cheat a feeble old lady.

Frank was Ray's lawyer for the business for nearly twenty

years, a savvy soul who says I must comply. To resist is to risk breaching the "cooperation clause" in the contact. The insurance company would enjoy nothing better.

Kate said it took less than an hour to bulldoze and cart the house away.

6.17.33 is engraved inside Mother's ring. Every day's an anniversary.

OLLIE HAS ASKED me to move into his place if this insurance matter keeps us here past the end of the month. By then I'll be out of another little home anyway. I seem to be excelling at this drift, without talent. But I hope not to have to drop my suitcases beside his bed here. I'll admit it. The idea of us both entering more spacious, more neutral, faraway ground for the start of our daily basis has appealed to me as a growing sanity. It might make us muses longer. Me to him, I hope.

Fortunately, he's gobbled up for the next two or three days in the pursuit of viruses in a steel company's inventory programs.

Thrilling.

Lucky he owns only about six shirts worth packing, two of which I bought him.

Quite awhile ago the Monster left a phone message saying the insurance investigator had interviewed him about the fire. He thought it was good to let them know he'd been away when it started.

That's the Monster. He doesn't often realize how things might otherwise appear.

The last number he dialed me from is still on my cell memory. I could try it. Maybe it's connected to an actual place where he is.

How long do I have anyway?
Who believes that, whatever they claim?
I've lived free and clear compared to that man chasing viruses.
There's no way to tell him what that means to me.
I think now he's lied about his age.
Ends on the loose.

KATE WAS SUPPOSED to meet me at Blue Jay Trail but canceled. A hangover, she said, from a night out with her peace activist group. But I believe it's a Stephen quandary edging in. Kate drank and smoked dope early on, ending one bout sprawled on a teeter-totter sixty miles out of town, she admitted, at fifteen. (You can guess the rest of how she was spitting herself away then, as kids will do.) But she quit it all, I think, because her sister Kelli wouldn't think twice about the destination. And she was blessed by the example of her father.

I see now I'd planned to stop with her at Terri's bench, about a mile down the trail, beside the fat cottonwood. "In loving memory of Terri Holman, 1966–2000," says the commemorative plate on the back. "She would have loved this spot." I've taken a break there, on occasion, wondering, as I guess we're supposed to, where she is and who grasped so well her unfelt feelings.

I see I would have given Kate my mother's ring there, and that I assumed she would be grateful. I see that I believed I knew what it would mean to her, as though I couldn't remember my mother thought she understood what she was doing. That's the nature of giving. Who could bear to give, otherwise?

I passed a mom pushing her two boys strapped into a buggy

down the pavement. She was wearing roller skates and looked to be a couple of states to the other side of nutty. Which means merely young and trying so hard. Her thighs have always been good and will be, it's obvious, even without the Roller Derby. But she can't be told that any more than those high-waisted teenagers, so slumped their boobs tumble into their hips, can be convinced to go vertical at all costs.

The skating mom . . . I guess I think of Jane among her brood in the special playroom she dogged Petey to have built. The barrels of crayons. And the glue and the glitter strewn everywhere. The bags of ice cream sticks (or tongue depressors) for building little projects. Our kids (everyone's kids) used to have to save them from their Bomb Pops and Creamsicles until they had enough to make something, maybe a trinket box. Now all the Janes can buy them by the gross.

You can't blame them for wanting to boost their kids' aptitudes, can you?

It's just a pity they don't let the Kates and Kellis into that wonderful room, too, especially since those girls hardly had a place to lay their heads half the time, let alone possess a Game Boy that could bore them until they tossed it. Petey and Jane were too scared their little ones would meet a bad influence (even from Grandma).

There was no justification to keep those kids separated. Cousins, after all.

———

But I've detoured from Terri's bench.

Actually, a woman was crouching there. At first I thought she was sick. But, no, she was watching a beetle (at least we think it was a beetle) digging itself out of the ground, being born, perhaps.

She was intent. It turns out she was desperate to be intent.

As we watched the beetle, she said she'd taken a personal day from her job at a bank. (She's a loan officer.) She passes Blue Jay Trail every day, she said, and she'd vowed to herself to stop but never had.

Her father died several months ago, and she wasn't getting over it.

She was suffering, I think, because all her family and friends had finally heard enough.

It was fresh in her.

I think I could sense this by how it felt like a sink full of marble plates in me so near her.

We sat on the bench, and she turned her face up to the sun as though she'd never done that before. She was intent on tearing the beauty out of everything and smearing it all over herself to hold herself together.

Something like that.

Every now and then April says, "Dad isn't dead," and I don't ask what she means by that, but you can guess. She decorates Ray's stone each Memorial Day. She stays close to that feeling, too close, however it changes. It's one she recognizes and believes she understands.

My daughter, who dressed a roadkill buck last winter with a saw because Howard was out of town. Can you believe her?

I mentioned April and Ray, and the young woman (she was maybe thirty-five) still had it in her to make sure I understood it was a comfort to hear this.

It wasn't, of course. So I tried to not offer further help of that sort.

We lingered there for a few more minutes, mainly because it was so beautiful, stunning, really, and we were deciding somehow that we weren't going to introduce ourselves.

T HE PHLEBITIS IN my toe has sneaked back slightly, thanks to fine clots my heart is throwing from a flap my surgeon says he'll need to darn sooner than later. The toe is swollen a little. I imagine red silt. But I send down the pill that brushes it away. Keep walking, the doc counsels, stay active. So I should be, instead of reading backwards over most of these pages this morning.

I guess I've reminisced.

I have too many memories sometimes for insight.

And it's easier to talk to you than any god. No god gets to be alive and die like we do.

You were an introduction. As you get older, things don't impress you as much, or you fear that.

I've never been one ready to give up my guilt for being merely misguided.

I turned to you.

Or into you.

Yeah. Still getting away with it.

So I have a lover now (imagine!) who's not so ancient everybody around us is on height-watch, monitoring for spine shrinkage. And I understand enough history now to realize why he sobbed as he did in bed on Afternoon Number Two, a tremendous clobbering, and the more the tears hammered and he shuddered, the greater the erection that seemed to present itself to us both, the most untamable address I'd encountered since my high school prom.

But I'm a little distressed by how much of who he is has missed appearing here. Or how much of Ray. Or anyone.

It's just as quiet in this room as it was two months ago, but I'm less troubled by it. Probably because I'm not leaving here in a box. (Mother bragged to me once in her last months, "I'm doing well. I was alone today for three hours!")

When a plane I'm riding in lifts off, I feel forgiven. That's one way of life I've indulged.

I mean, it's about time to let go of this nonsense. It's done its duty. You and the rest will survive it. Even the little rolled-up and burned hairs on Ray's knees (knee-dreadlocks, from our cheap just-married sheets, which I trimmed off with a fingernail clipper) will survive it.

Funny, I just remembered again Ollie's book of photographs from a museum in Mexico, one picture of a tribal woman whose breasts are bared. The caption said they'll be covered only on her wedding day and when she dies.

I guess she'll survive it, too.

Kate declares the only truth is made up. At least, that's what she was taught this spring in a class at the community college. (Not much different from what they reveal in the dowdy brick church across Pleasant Hill Road, except over there God has let them know he makes it up.)

So isn't it probably transparent why people have pets they can talk love to, simply, maybe even in secret, and it won't be thrown back at them?

I wonder what truth she's making up about Stephen and those bruises on her arms.

Rather than charging hard into a walk today, I think I'll try the driving range. I haven't taken a swing since September. And it occurs to me I've never gone there alone.

Then to April's, if the sun's still out.

SHELBY INTRODUCED ME to Stretch-pants Man, since they happened to be grilling on his porch. His name is actually Rodger Malatesta. He played Little Ike on the TV western *Gold Rush!*, which ran for a couple of seasons in the early sixties. Rodger was shocked, and pleased, I remembered it so well. (Shelby had never heard of it when he'd told her. Too young.) But I'd sat through a lot of TV in those days I was living in the dump on Walnut Avenue and leaving you constantly in Chicago. I could probably chart the history of my Drears by the shows that took me in (though I read my way through some of those epochs, between naps).

You wouldn't believe (when I come to think of it) what TV is now.

It seems like the fate of every hillside and daydream depends on it, though there's still not much of life in the thing. (You'd have had plenty to say about all those images, I think. Pity, again.)

Anyway, reruns of *Gold Rush!* pop up now and then on cable, which is probably also why my memory of it is moderately fresh.

Shelby's very proud.

I wonder how many times that's been Rodger's good luck, if it ever has been?

Also, April called to inform me that Ray's sister Grace expects Ollie and me to appear at the Lundgrove Memorial Day Picnic this weekend, out at her place. News of Ollie has found the outmost gossips of Guthrie County, apparently. She wants to ascertain for herself. So I'd better prepare him for an afternoon of pinochle with the family fogies. It's a Lundgrove game. Ray's mother used to make us play by the hour while she talked and talked about everyone out of sight.

T HE INSURANCE COMPANY took my testimony under oath yesterday. Fortunately, Frank Garcia prepped me for the grilling (as Petey called it, quite miffed for me at first).

They dug down into my figures, accounts and debts and whatnot, as Frank assured me they would. They peel you skillfully, like some rotten fruit they have to check for blight. And they enjoy their task.

More than once, I had to remember Ollie's dragon-discipline, whatever it is, since they wanted to get to me, and I can be gotten to.

But I answered everything straightaway, mostly because Frank emphasized I had nothing to lose.

I did, of course. Petey was shocked to hear about my two other bank accounts. I've let him run my affairs, blessedly, to the extent he's needed to know them. He's bruised now. Again. The mess is there in the silence around his sigh like a heavy bed just dragged one last inch to scar the floor.

In the end, I came off as I am. A woman with a backwards live-in son who's lost her house. Hardly rich but more than solvent and a little fey (which, to be truthful, I'm catching myself at being, more and more).

Frank reminded the creatures deposing me that our investigator offers a different interpretation of the fire.

The physical evidence is so contradictory, Frank says, and my testimony removed any possibility that I needed to light up for money. They'll pay.

I guess I will, too.

I TRIED THE MOST recent Monster number on my cell phone memory.

I thought I could attempt to thank him for Mother's ring (and, chucking the obvious question of whose finger it's been on lately, suggest that perhaps it would make a better gift to his daughter—though that wouldn't work, I soon realized).

I deserve to announce I'm going, if he hasn't heard. (I'm sure I've spotted Cane Toad's pickup cruising these environs at least twice this week. But who can you report that disquieting phenomenon to? Believe me, I scan the lot before I step out to my car.)

The number turned out to be for Billing's Body Shop on 2nd Avenue. The woman's voice said, "He isn't here anymore."

August 22, 2004
Mr. Oliver Picks
16 Brushy Road
Piper Lake, Michigan 49801

Dear Mr. Picks--

You may not remember me since we only met a couple of times but I'm Jill Lundgrove's granddaughter. I'm sending you these pages written by Granna last year because she mentions you so much in them and she loved you its clear and I have the feeling you maybe don't know about them. Also because I'm sure my Uncle Pete doesn't want anyone to see them. He is very protective!

After Granna left town with you last summer, I got her old computer and this writing was in the trash on it. I think she thought she'd deleted it but that's not the case. It was under the file name Letter to Beaut. I began reading it not knowing what it was and couldn't stop. (I guess I've always been nosy.)

Anyway, after Granna was gone and since the computer

had been my Uncle Pete's I took the file to him (after making a copy for myself obviously). I almost didn't but what could I do really? I told him I'd read it first because I didn't know what it was (which was true) and then I'd kept it quiet because it wasn't my business to begin with. He made me promise not to tell anyone else about it. At the time I didn't know if anyone should see it. I'd thought of putting some quotes from it on Granna's memorial webpage. They would certainly make it more personal, but I couldn't find things that were appropriate.

I hope you are finding peace in your cabin and are not hurting too much for being alone there. I think of you waking up and finding Granna. I don't know how a person does that. When my dad died, I was so angry I couldn't even cry. Now I've started learning to meditate. I go to a class with my sort of fiancé Stephen (who's dealing with some big challenges, too). We've been reading When Things Fall Apart by Pema Chodron, about bodhichitta "the noble or awakened heart." Chodron says "in the midst of loneliness, in the midst of fear, in the middle of feeling misunderstood and rejected is the heartbeat of all things, the genuine heart of sadness." Not hiding from suffering is the way to heal. That's what she says.

Anyway, I hope Granna's diary will help with your pain if that's the case. Its helped me. I read it often last fall trying to figure out what is obviously a complicated life, definitely not a book like its cover. I used to wonder what I would think and how I would act with her next time I saw her. Who'd have guessed? It was weird. I was afraid she'd be able to tell somehow that I'd read it. Now when I reread passages I see her face, and I think maybe she wanted someone to know it. God I can almost hear her saying these things. Funny since she didn't really talk like she does there. To me at least.

Anyway, good wishes to you. I know I can trust you will keep this confidential.

Yours Truly,
Kate Lundgrove

May 20, 2004
Eleanor Hokin
519 Sea Chart Lane
Sanibel Island, Florida 33957

Dear Ms. Hokin:

I'm afraid I'm writing with bad news. My mother, Jill Lundgrove, died this spring in her sleep, apparently of a massive coronary. She had been staying with friends in the Upper Peninsula of Michigan and was found in the morning, when she didn't come down to breakfast. You may know that she had suffered from some coronary problems recently and had a pacemaker implanted last year. Though the prognosis from the procedure was good, and her health was otherwise fairly sound, anything can happen, especially since my mother, always stubborn, as you know, refused to quit smoking. So we must not be entirely surprised.

This sorrow has come on the heels of the sudden loss of my brother Monte last June. I'm sure you heard about it. He was found shot to death, probably the result of criminal misdealing, according to the police. Monte's death weighed heavily on my mother, and no doubt it strained her. Further, as you may know, about the time of her first coronary problems she had suffered the loss of her house to a fire that consumed nearly everything of value. Truly, it had been a challenging time, and we are all still reeling.

Now, in going through her few surviving personal effects, we realize how much was lost in that fire, how little remains for keepsakes and the like. We have memories, of course, and we are sharing stories, trying to piece together all that we can.

That's why we hope you can help shed some light on one of the items we found. The original copy of the enclosed letter was among papers in a box that had somehow survived the fire. The handwriting on the envelope is the same as on the letter itself. "Beaut the Smuggler" was written on the envelope. Obviously, it was never intended to be sent through the mail. And the envelope itself was still sealed. It appears my mother never opened it.

Included with this document were two photographs of my mother as a young woman, very skillful photos, I might add, though semi-pornographic.

Do you know who wrote this letter? Or who took the pictures? We have no name, nothing. You're the only person we can think of from that time whom we can contact and who might know.

To say the least, it is strange to think of our mother as the adventurous person who posed for such pictures. As you may recall, my sister April and I are adopted. We have few memories of our birth mother. Jill was our true mother and our world.

If you have any information at all about these documents or about that time, please contact me at the email address or toll-free office number below.

Any help you can give the family would be greatly appreciated. Again, I'm sorry to bring you this news.

Sincerely,

Peter Lundgrove

Dearest B,

By now, you know. I'm sorry you do, this way. Please don't forgive me, if that helps. I deserve worse. A few days after we met, the wolf came back. It had been a long time since it had shown up. I thought it might be gone for good. I thought maybe I might have left it back in KC, under grandma's bed or somewhere. I thought it might get lost again since we started running together. It had nothing to do with you.

The other night you saw it jump into me. It was a terrible shock, I know. I would never hurt you. Believe me. I can never be sorry enough.

There's no place for me with it near. There's never been any time to explain it. Don't think this is the coward's way out. I love you. I've burned all my poetry for you. I've burned all my negatives and prints except these two.

You helped me try for the art I hoped for. Who did I think I was? Everything hurts very much. You in this print, so sweetly sidewise, so very fine, your chin on your knee. You trusted me. How could you have known I was the enemy, the silver-suited schemer? You've scared me more than anything with your courage. Just to see you ask me what's wrong. It's no use. I can hardly lift this pen. You deserve better and you'll get it. I should have broken things off months ago instead of sitting down for you. This isn't what I meant. But it's where I'm turning. I can't stand this voice anymore. Please. It's better now than later. Better to know less and be free.

Love Always,
B

6.9.04

Dear Peter—

I'm shocked to hear the terrible news about your mother. I
loved her like a little sister. I'm also very saddened to hear
of Monte's passing. I remember him so well. He tried to be
a good son, and I know there were difficult times for him.
Thank God, Jill had you at hand.

    My eyes are very poor now, so I am able only to write
these cards. I had my neighbor read me the strange letter
you inquired about. I'm afraid it doesn't ring any bells, and I
don't know who might know anything about it. So many of
our group are already gone, too soon. But it doesn't surprise
me that your mother had been involved in artistic things
somewhere or that she kept this quiet. From the moment
we met, you could tell she didn't see the world the way most
people do, or thought she didn't, and for some reason she
always tried to pretend she did.

I'm sorry. Good luck in your search. Please let me know if you find out something.

My heartfelt sympathy to you and all your family.

Eleanor Hokin

July 22, 2004
Carla Freeborne
11245 Pomello Road
Santa Fe, New Mexico 89505

Dear Car,

Here's Mom's writing from the apartment. As I said on the
phone, it's full of provocative stuff. Laugh if you must, but I
really had to pray on whether or not to bother you with it.

Just remember, as you read, that she was never quite right
after her collapse. The doctor had her on one prescription
that, I discovered later, is also given to Alzheimer's patients.
She also had too much time on her hands in that apartment.
That's my fault. But you know how stubborn she was, and
putting her there was the only hope to finally get her away
from Monte's mess.

Also, you should receive, via certified mail, those
documents we discussed. I checked with Mom's lawyer, and
it's just as you suspected. Picks has no rights to anything,
since her will is in force and she has no community property

beyond the vacant lot. I had Mom's lawyer phone him and inform him of that. Apparently, he said he had no interest in the matter. Strange fellow. I was sure he'd talked her into getting married up there because he'd discovered she actually had some assets. Why else would they have kept it secret?

At any rate, please sign the documents and return them via certified mail right away. As you well know, the sooner they're filed the sooner the estate can be settled. April is alternately catatonic over Mom and weirdly suspicious that she won't receive her full share. I think we can attribute the latter emotions to pressure from Howard.

About Mom's writing: To be honest, I'm not eager to see it passed around. I think it would only create more problems. And haven't we had enough of those?

When you finish reading it, let's talk. Okay?

Love to you,
Petey

P.S. I can't believe you still hadn't told Mom that you and Karen took the same last name!

SUBJECT: The Saga Continues
DATE: Friday, October 1, 2004 11:12:17 AM
FROM: CFreeborne@DDBNA.com
TO: Plundgrove@RPDairies.com

Petey, I know it's been too long since you gave me our mother's "testament" and I haven't responded. To be honest, I'm uncertain when I'll be able to read it all. I started on it, but after a few pages, I had to stop.

As far as I'm concerned, how much is fiction here and how much we should bother to trust as fact is very much in question. Right away, she acknowledges she lies (as though we didn't know that already). So do I really want to hear her further commentaries on you or me, or anyone? Do I have to listen to her justify herself or Monte again? Do I need to hear about her romances or, for god's sake, her sexual practices?

I have no idea who she's really addressing here, Pete, or what she's up to, and, frankly, I'm unwilling to undertake the task of figuring that out. Even though this document was in the trash on her computer, do you believe she didn't want you to find it? She always had to have the final word, even if it was a sigh. I just can't allow her that again, not like this.

You know it was always all about her. The way she treated Dad. (I can remember him telling me, more than once, long before he became ill, "Your mother is special, she can't help that, so go easy on her.") And there she was, cleaning out his drawers and bagging his clothes the day before the funeral.

And this isn't even to begin to mention, yet again, how, in spite of everyone, she managed to help Monte ruin himself. They were a pair, weren't they, to the end?

You could call her a frustrated actress only if you didn't realize she was acting all the time.

I did all the pleasing I could do, Petey, just as you have. I've done all the forgiving I can. Who says we have to do more, simply because she's gone?

Karen, by the way, has endured plenty as I've worked through these issues over the years, and she's been so kind and patient she doesn't deserve to have to deal with it all yet again. We're in a good place now. I let old demons ruin one marriage. Not again.

You didn't mention in your note whether you'd given April a copy or not. It would seem fair she deserves a chance to see this thing. On the other hand, given the obviously unfounded, embarrassing and potentially damaging subject matter, and since our mother didn't technically intend the document as part of her estate, I don't think we're obligated, as her co-executors, to make its existence known.

Actually, writing this to you has already helped me come to what seems the best solution. I just put the document through my office shredder.

Please let that be it. I can't bring this thing up anymore. Sorry.

Love to you,
Car-Car

SUBJECT: RE: The Saga Continues
DATE: Friday, October 1, 2004 1:12:12 PM
FROM: Plundgrove@RPDairies.com
TO: CarlaFreeborne@DDBNA.com

Done!

OX

Dear Kate:

Thank you for your grandmother's remarkable diary--what a gift! I'm surprised . . . and yet not surprised, given the shy, powerful spirit she sometimes opened to people.

I'm deeply grateful for your kindness--to be frank, I thought I'd never hear from anyone in your family again. I assume your Uncle Peter has slandered me at every opportunity.

Please understand that I didn't attend the funeral because before I could complete the arrangements to transport your grandmother's body to Des Moines, your Uncle Peter and Aunt Carla arrived here and took over.

Peter was furious with grief, and he had to be in charge of her-- he more or less commanded me to stay away.

I had no real business in this, he said--imagine that!

We argued, especially when they came to the house, expecting to simply take whatever of hers they wanted--in the end, I tried to imagine how your grandmother might handle the situation and decided that my presence in Des Moines would only make a difficult moment more tense for everyone.

I could hear her chuckle and say "My body won't know if you're a hundred feet away or a thousand miles."

But I've kicked myself every day for giving in to that voice--a couple of our friends here helped me offer a small ceremony for her on the dock at sunset (what she called her favorite sad hour), but it's never the same.

Rest assured I'll keep this diary as our secret treasure--it will give me solace, I'm sure, through the coming days, which already grow shorter and colder. (I've gotten rid of my place in Des Moines, by the way, and have decided to remain here for the foreseeable.)

In the spirit of your generous gesture, I've sent you, via snail mail, Xerox copies of pages in her handwriting that I'd kept back as mementos. A couple of times, when I happened upon her composing like that, I'd offered to get her a new computer, so she could do email, etc--it would have been terribly simple. But she declined, saying she wasn't ready "to jack back into the world yet." She spent a lot of the winter reading Russian novels and watching movies and prodding me to walk around the lake with her, which I did when it seemed she truly wanted company--I think we were both surprised we kept staying on here through those white months.

A few of the pages are addressed explicitly to you--as you'll see, none are numbered, or dated, but obviously they're recent.

I've also included in the package your great-grandmother's wedding ring--I'm sure Jill meant to give it to you before we left Des Moines, had your father's death not consumed her attention. She

169

spoke of you often with such deep affection, and she was always elated after chatting with you on the phone.

I've come to believe we're rarely allowed to choose our tokens-- that's why they sometimes strengthen us as much as they do.

Good luck with your Buddhist practice, and with Stephen and the challenges.

I hope you keep up your activism, too--your grandmother was proud of that in you.

Again, many, many thanks.

Ollie

PLEASE THINK HARD about having that child just now. Motherhood is a wonderful thing, people will tell you, but you know from your own experience how difficult it can be, especially for a very young woman who hasn't finished her education. Can you see that in your mother? It's there.

I mean, sometimes we try to do a better job than our parents did. We try to somehow correct their faults by living a certain way. That's a mistake you don't usually see until it's very late, too late. I love you, Kate, and I want the best for you. So understand this when I say you have so much more growing up to do, so much more to see and experience before you take on those kinds of obligations. Give yourself a chance. I don't know what Stephen thinks about the situation, but he needs that same chance.

I'm sure others are speaking to you about this. Do I sound like them? If so, I regret it, because a high-spirited young woman like you isn't likely to listen to advice from a crowd. I didn't.

~~A long time ago, when I was only a little older than you are now, I had to face the same decision. I've never told anyone about this, Kate, and~~

Well

OW DID I get here, with the moon out there on the other side of the glass?

Your father's out there now, if he's anywhere. And he can see me, too, if they can see. Maybe he can see now how difficult it is for us all. Though he probably could see that anyway.

He told me once, in one of his straight and narrow periods after detox, "Dad had to die to be close to me."

We understand that, don't we?

Your Uncle Peter once told me, "Sick as Dad was, he was here, at the house, and my days had to point toward visiting him. When he was finally gone, he was suddenly with me all the time."

That, too.

~~I must tell you~~ That afternoon on Blue Jay Trail, when your father begged me for that money, I couldn't believe him. Not after everything, not just then. And I know you believe me in this. We'd both stood by him through so many disasters. You would have said no, too.

$10,000!

I should have guessed by the ridiculous amount that he really was in trouble with people who were going to hurt him if he didn't pay up. Unfortunately, I'm letting this idea pervade me now.

But who can know?

~~Your father could cry the tears in me I didn't dare. I think that's what turned me his way so often. He was mine and never mine, but we couldn't understand this properly. I always, always realized he was wrong and mostly didn't deserve~~

You'll discover this, one day, if you haven't already. Of course, you have.

I suppose you saw that in me a long while ago.

When he was about eight, your father asked me, "Mom, what's inside a snake?"

That was him, too.

But probably not enough. (Or too much?)

~~Am I truthful because he's out there with the moon? Or the wine~~

————

I'd brought my checkbook with me that day, in my fanny pack. He'd probably supposed I'd bring it, which made me feel like a spigot.

When hadn't I given over at least part of what he'd sworn he needed?

As I told the police, I thought he'd figured the insurance company had paid, and so the auspicious moment to work me had arrived. Of course, that's where my mind was. And one more reason I insisted we meet in public. I couldn't judge what kind of shape he was in. Who could? And I didn't want to be alone with him.

~~For a minute, I thought of asking you to come with me. Right away, I understood that wouldn't be fair to any of us. But then again you~~ I was still worried about him learning where I lived even then, though I'd more or less vacated the place. Funny, too, since the apartment address was on my checks, anyway, and Cane Toad had cased the area several times, sure as cruelty.

Your father could hardly walk a hundred feet down the trail from the parking lot before his arm was around my shoulders to herd me to a bench. You know that weight. He looked so mealy and nervous, I didn't realize then that he probably needed to keep us in sight of Cane Toad in the SUV. Or, more likely, in sight of the people in the back seat of the SUV who had put Cane Toad behind their wheel. (It certainly wasn't Cane Toad's vehicle.) That's the problem. Any of us can imagine all kinds of movie thugs, there in that back seat. These days, I recall Cane Toad staring at me strangely, from a very formal distance, as though he were stricken in his backbone. Was he that terrified? I can't say the possibility hurts my heart even now very much, since he's still among the living, if you can call living what apparently engages him.

~~But when I first got out of my car there, I understood I shouldn't approach him. Not that I would have been attracted otherwise.~~

Your father told me straight out that he'd made some serious mistakes, more serious than ever before, but that when this was over, he would never let himself be put in this position again. He explained how it was in the interest of my safety to keep me out of the details.

In other words, the usual, elaborated, or so it seemed, and maybe was.

I told him I was leaving town, that we might not have contact for a long time, if ever.

~~I'd decided beforehand that I needed to say this. I was still amazed to hear it.~~

My words didn't register on him. They didn't make enough contact for disregard. I don't think it was any of the ample drug effect that prevented this, or his anxiety.

He just stared at me. As though I hadn't spoken.

I'd sounded as phony to myself as he did to me. That didn't change our bargain.

I wrote a check.

I didn't dare not. It felt like my little window out of that dungeon.

What I didn't tell the police, or anyone, is that before I filled in the amount, I believed I wanted the truth: Did he purposely burn down my house?

This registered.

He laughed but then glanced at the checkbook in my lap and sombered. ~~I'd never encountered a~~

"I want an answer," I said. I touched his hand, and he pulled it away.

"These past months haven't been easy for me," I said. "It will help me to know."

A good parent reputedly rewards a child's honesty. But what does a parent do when her darling spikes it?

Your father ever so softly said, "Yes." And also that he was "full of remorse" and that it was only because things had "gotten out of hand" that the fire started, but "this was no excuse" for the wrong he'd done me.

I suppose I deserved that performance.

I filled in the check. $500.

I could have made it out for more, even the whole $10,000, ugly as that would have been for my balance.

"That's all I can do right now," I said.

I made sure to emphasize that "right now."

I held out the check to him.

That's when he sobbed. Bereft. ~~For a second I almost believed he~~

But he was helpless, I thought, like the day he left me on the floor. And I had to remember that.

I owe you my life, dear. ~~That's why I'm trying this out, here. Your mother would~~

I'm trying to find something worthy to give you back for it.

I expect you to understand that, but I'm being unfair again.

~~I should speak with you about these things. We've almost managed that, so often. Talk would be better than this. Or maybe it But there are so many ways to misunderstand~~

I've nagged Detective Roberts so often he should receive a therapist's license. He insists there's no evidence our meeting had anything to do with the murder. There's no evidence involving Cane Toad. No SUV thugs. Nothing.

When I'm weak, I don't believe him.

When I'm weak, I see myself holding out a piece of paper to my son, that he could grab to pull himself free from the crumbling edge of a vast pit, a piece of paper that with some other ink scratches on it, just a few other scratches, would make the difference.

~~The point is~~

Having this baby won't bring your father back.

You understand that.

Don't you?

What can I do about it if you don't?

~~You're in the time of life of love notes dashed off in silver ink.~~
~~Your father~~

———

Talking of your grandfather—someone you barely remember. That's part of life, too. Perhaps most of it. People you barely know, or don't remember, influence you. We're often haunted without realizing we're accompanied. Many frustrated ghosts around. Maybe they're the most effective ones, if ghosts wish to be effective.

They—the younger—they're eager. They want the sex, they want the car, they want the old cat put to sleep . . . they don't know anything about anticipation, or patience, or a frozen grip.

We repeat ourselves (and many others) long before we're old, before we become aware we're judged for it. The young think they don't repeat. That's how you know someone, whatever their age, is still a child, or has become one again.

THE JAYS AND many colorless birds hack at the corn cobs Ollie stuffs on the vertical spindles out back. You'd think we'd contracted with them years ago for this, since they appeared seconds after he put the stuff out. Ollie hasn't been to this place in three years, but it's the same with the cobs now, he says, as it was when he was a boy. There are rituals. Which is why for the first month here he'd only drink the cheap beer from the lake store. It's a hut, really, like the one at Panorama. Do you remember our place? Like there, the store seems to have three cans of charcoal starter on the shelf, some dusty ginger snaps and fishing lures and beef jerky. And the cheap beer. That's all the civilization required, apparently.

Ollie's house is a low-slung thing, with two bedrooms, all knotty pine inside and a huge stone fireplace, which we started using some nights in August and all the time now. The screened porches are rusty and cozy, and the coffee cups are thick-walled and chipped just right. And among the stones in the chimney, there's a large one in the middle, about eye-level, that's shaped exactly like a valentine heart. Every day I wonder where the builder (who was the first owner) found it and how long he kept it separated from the rest until he found that special placement.

Most of all, of course, is the water, just beyond the side porch. Ollie baits the fish hooks. I never could shove a living worm along that steel. But he's taught me to clean the catch. I've had to buck up. I'll admit the cheap beer helps.

We've already seen snow flurries disappear into water, and the few leaves that can change, have. (Which is good. The chill keeps the flies down.) The evenings still sometimes smell sweet and fresh, of fish just at the moment they're caught. It's lovelier here than the pictures on the postcards I've sent. One morning, I watched a gull skirt the glassy surface. But, no, the actual bird was higher up. I'd been following a reflection, and it seemed to dip more deeply into the mirror as the gull ascended.

If we're here in the spring, you might want to visit. Maybe even for Christmas. I don't think we're going to travel soon. It was enough effort to get up here, after everything. Driving in separate cars for three days, staring at the back of Ollie's head. I thought I was crazy at least a hundred times.

We're peaceful, here. Even though Ollie's tomcat, Sominex, is dismally house-bound since he's eagle-bait. Even though every day is a weird start we must be kind to.

~~I hope going back to school continues to excite your~~
~~Crows had chopped holes in the roof for nests and~~
~~I'm glad you've been able to give your mother some comfort.~~
~~She and your father were together too long for her feelings to~~
~~have~~

I RESPECT YOUR PRIVACY, Kate, but anyone could spot those bruises on your arms. And no makeup could conceal that spot on your chin. They weren't part of a hangover from your peace group, we understand that.

I know my share about fearing a man, maybe a man you love, a man like Stephen. It's not good to stay with someone who's hurt you and who could hurt you again, worse. Just as a woman and her best girlfriend don't have to climb into a car with strangers who blindfold them for the drive to the abortion hideout anymore (the way of the world when I was your age), there are places to get help for an abusive relationship. Of course you know this. Everyone knows this. But that doesn't mean any one woman understands it's her time to move.

———

I probably sound old-fashioned, don't I? After all, dear, I have you to thank for getting me to finally come out of my routines. I wouldn't have met Ollie. I wouldn't have discovered I needed to wave a peace placard, that it would feel so right but unsettling, too, like the day you touch your belly and realize it will never be tight with child again.

———

Long before I met your grandfather, I went off to seek my fortune in Chicago. This was 1959–1960. I suppose in some ways it was a time of adventuring like this one with Ollie, except that I thought I hadn't lived. I was willing, eager for experience. Like you.

I met a man. He washed dishes to pay the rent. But his goal was to be a photographer, an artist, really, and he was. He took beautiful pictures. He wrote poetry, too. He'd read hugely, and he had the most amazing friends. Being together was like dancing down a bright hallway lined with doors to open to sparkling planets and perfumes and wide-eyed ideas and laughter.

We became lovers. I tell you, Kate, nothing has ever tasted as good to me as him then.

But we'd been together only a while when things became strange. I'll admit it. We drank (and he drank too much). There was marijuana around, at some of the parties, too. But that wasn't it. He was slipping somehow, and it began to scare me.

I woke up one night at his place and found him sitting next to me in bed, cross-legged, watching me.

He'd told me he was studying my beauty. Which began to give me the creeps the more I thought about it.

Another time I came over to his place from work and let myself in and found him sitting on the window ledge with a knife in his lap. He seemed to be humming or singing to it, or to something. He wouldn't tell me. He said he was examining the light.

Maybe I should have foreseen. But what did I really know about him? He'd moved to Chicago from Kansas City to escape his family and become an artist. That was it. Not a surprise. And I was in love.

The end came when he tied me up.

I thought it was a game at first until he gagged me and drew a knife from the kitchen and put it on the table in front of me.

He took off all his clothes then and marched around, trying to confess to me, hysterical that I couldn't see his sin, naked as he was, that I couldn't see him.

He became enraged that I couldn't forgive him.

He picked up the knife and waved it around several times.

He pleaded with me. He shouted. He touched my hair, and I actually wet myself.

Finally, he lay down on the floor and went to sleep.

I've never told anyone this story, Kate. There was never a good enough reason to. I'm telling you because I'm still alive thanks only to your quick thinking, and I love you, and we've lost so much recently, and I worry about Stephen. From our phone calls, I sense there's something really wrong. I want you to know we can talk about it if you need to. Don't wait too long, as I did.

I'm probably telling you, too, because I need you to understand why I had to go away with Ollie now, why it was my only hope, and so it wasn't entirely selfish.

I stared at this man I thought I'd loved, there sleeping, curled up on the floor, and I tried to untie myself without rousing him.

When he woke up, he was emptied out, frightened. He tried first to apologize to me, but instead he just untied me. I ran out the front door. I remember shouting back, "You crazy sonofabitch!" I almost laughed it sounded so insufficient.

Maybe I should have called the police. But I couldn't untangle the situation, and I didn't have anyone I could trust with trying to.

He once said to someone who asked him what his pictures were about, "I'm performing an experiment in human motivation and betrayal."

Should I have understood?

For days after that horrible night I cried in my little apartment. I felt I'd lost everything, even though I was blessedly intact.

He called and called. I was never going to answer.

But here's the clutch. I did answer, finally.

He convinced me to come to his place after I got off work that evening, to say a final goodbye. That was the way we phrased it.

I knocked several times on his door. I should have turned and gone right then. But I let myself in.

I found him in bed, already cool and stiffening. He'd taken a huge number of pills. There were several empty prescription bottles on the nightstand.

The place was wire-neat, as it had never been, and so silent I could hear my sleeves. He'd even put my few things into a grocery bag next to the bed.

I sat beside him for awhile. I lay my head on his chest. There was a faint evening light along one edge of the window curtain, that gold.

Don't misunderstand me, Kate. He was a wonderful man, a boy, really. Sweet, complex, hurting. Remarkably talented.

But I had to leave him there alone.

It's not that there isn't life for you afterward, or no chance for love or happiness. (Though I won't say it helps much to wonder what else might fit in your heart if this or that thing wasn't there . . . or to wonder if you might have been keeping it there just to keep other things out.)

I suppose it's like the apple trees scattered around here, bare and very black now the snow is drifting. On the far tip of a branch high enough no deer can get to it and thin enough no squirrel can shimmy out on it, you find a single, shriveled fruit, a deep rust. You know it's floating in the one perfect space, a common thing growing rarer every second, until it's not even fruit anymore.

I bet it holds on until spring, for sure.

~~I mean it wasn't always such a long time ago, Kate. For many years, it was the only wrong to save me. But that's a story I'm just beginning to~~

Okay. So this letter isn't working out. I don't know what I'm doing. I have to try again. But later.

Now it's obviously more worthwhile to call and ask if the baby has moved today. Isn't it?

ACKNOWLEDGMENTS

Many thanks to Robin Miura and Lynn York of Blair for believing in this book and giving it their meticulous attention.

Thanks also to the University of Tampa for a Dana Summer Fellowship, which helped the work along, and to Robert and Barbara Strickler, for the use of their country place, where I found the momentum.

Most of all, my gratitude and love to Lisa Birnbaum, first reader, deep eye.